10t

RED
MOON

RED MOON

MOON

RACHEL ANDERSON

Hodder
Children's
Books

A division of Hachette Children's Books

A Catalogue record for this book is available from the British Library

ISBN-10: 0 340 79940 4
ISBN-13: 978 0 340 79940 6

Typeset in Frutiger and Bembo by Avon DataSet Ltd,
Bidford on Avon, Warwickshire

Printed and bound in Great Britain by
Bookmarque Ltd, Croydon, Surrey

The paper and board used in this paperback by Hodder Children's Books
are natural recyclable products made from wood grown in sustainable forests.
The manufacturing processes conform to the environmental
regulations of the country of origin.

Hodder Children's Books
a division of Hachette Children's Books
338 Euston Road
London NW1 3BH

Contents

SEA CHANGE

LANDFALL

WONDERLAND

TALES FROM SCHOOL

Hamish and the
Blood-sausage Butcher

Hamish was not like other boys. There were six reasons why.

1. He never played football. 2. His father was a knotty Scot. 3. His mother couldn't cook to save her life. 4. He suffered from asthma. 5. He had no friends. 6. He always handed in his homework on time.

One morning, near the lock-up shops on Paragon Parade, something occurred which confirmed that peculiar things happened to him that didn't happen to everybody.

His route was blocked by metal barriers. Red and white striped tape, marked Do Not Enter Do Not Enter Do Not Enter, stretched between them. The surly woman who ran the launderette was leaning on the metal barrier as though she was waiting to watch a horse race.

'If them bustards won't let an honest citizen open up

her Washeteria, I'm blowed if I'm hanging round here all morning while they make up their minds,' she muttered.

Who were the carrion she was referring to? There wasn't a soul about, though Mr Joel must have already arrived for his metal shutter was unlocked and half up. The bookie, the estate agent's and the DIY never opened before nine.

'*Who* won't make up their minds?'

'It'll be the foreigners again, won't it? Creating trouble for the rest of us who pay our way. So I'm off back to my burrow for the day. And if you take my advice, you'll do the same.'

'I have to go to school,' said Hamish reasonably.

'Suit yourself. But you don't want to get yourself mixed up in their sort of trouble. You should see some of the things those women bring in to wash. What they wear under their big drapes is no mystery to me, I can tell you.' And she waddled away.

Hamish remained resolutely by the barrier. He'd been off school with another respiratory attack yet had, nonetheless, completed his homework. He must hand it in in time for it to be awarded the grades he knew he deserved. Despite his disability he was no dingbat.

If he squeezed round the barrier he could sidle rapidly down the pavement. However, what if the closure of the thoroughfare was for a sound reason? Gas leak? Unexploded bomb? MP's visit? His life had, so far, been uneventful apart from asthma attacks. He could think of no further excuses for closing off a pedestrian street.

He'd have to go to the bus stop by the alternative route. Go back three blocks, skirt round the park, scary territory ruled by slurred drunks and aggressive ne'er-do-wells (as his father called them). Anticipating the long walk made him reach nervously for his inhaler. He could become breathless from overexertion before he'd even moved a muscle.

A dark-uniformed figure was suddenly crouching beside him. The top half of its face was hidden behind the visor of a helmet. 'Get down! Get back! Get down!'

Having a mouth order you about when you can't see the eyes is spooky. Hamish obeyed. Immediately, a whole team of them leaped out of nowhere. All in riot gear, fatigue pants, big boots, body-protection vests, leather gauntlets, visored helmets. Like a streak of navy-blue lightning, they ran along the pavement to the butcher's.

The leader clicked some quiet commands, then shouted that whoever was hiding inside was to come out. Hamish saw Mr Joel raise his arms. In alarm, or surrender? It was hard to see through the metal shutter.

Mr Joel was a mild, old-fashioned butcher. He prepared all his own sausages, black puddings, chopped-liver-and-herb faggots, pressed muzzle, marinade tripe, chitterlings. Some mornings, Hamish saw him struggle in with the sides of beef, half lambs, bags of pigs' blood for making the blutwurst. Hamish wasn't a vegetarian so he didn't mind. The only item he couldn't bear was the lungs, white and flaccid, reminding him of his own feeble organs. If the butcher spotted Hamish, he would dart out with a gift.

'For you, mein herr! See, such just a tiny smidgeon! To munch on your motorbus! To keep strong your brains.' And he would hold out a sample of that day's speciality sausage on a wooden toothpick. Mr Joel was always pressing. It was impossible to refuse his gift, even though it meant going to school with pork grease leaking through the lining of his blazer pocket.

But today, no free samples. Mr Joel stood, hands up inside his shop while, with a cacophony like clanging bells, the raiders rammed at the front shutter with an instrument like the barrel of a cannon. They dented it but failed to force it up so swarmed under like blue ferrets.

Hamish was squatting by the barrier, stupefied as a dog in a thunderstorm, when the team swaggered out.

Now their visors were pushed back. Hamish saw happy eyes, smiles of satisfaction.

'So. Nothing,' one said with a grin. 'False lead. Ha ha.'

The leader snapped commands into the radio-stick clipped to his helmet. The heavyman lifted the battering ram lightly onto his shoulder like a woodsman bringing home a log for the hearth, and the team trotted off like children playing Down into the Dingly Dell. At the end of the street their transport van nosed round the corner. They scrambled in and were gone. The whole escapade was through in minutes. The grey parade was quiet.

Hamish crept to the butcher's. The shutter hung lopsided. Hamish dipped under.

Mr Joel stood, hands limp, in his wrecked shop, shaking his head. The mirror behind the counter was cracked. Hamish saw his own misaligned reflection and behind it, distorted chaos. The cold-store door at the back swung open. Half sides of pig, sheep, cow, dragged from their hooks in the cool dark, lay like savaged victims on the floor. A stainless-steel trayful of lambs' livers slid along the sloping shelf, clattered to the sawdust. Hamish jumped, too late to avoid the crimson splatter.

'What's going on?' he asked.

The butcher shrugged. 'Indeed, what? Perhaps an erroneous betrayal? One customer is not liking my blood sausage? He tried to spill the beans. He spilled the meat.' Mr Joel smiled at his little joke.

Hamish said, 'Seriously, what were they looking for?'

'Turks. Always searching for the Turks.'

'Why here?'

'How am I knowing this? Nobody is knowing the names of the sans-papiers. They work like slaves in Germany, these poor lonesome men speaking no German, then hope it is better here. The authorities like to poke the thumb at me because I speak German and make good blutwurst.'

Mr Joel's use of English could be as unusual as Hamish's mother's. Sometimes, when Anne-Marie came with Hamish to buy a slice of black pudding, she would unconsciously break into Alsace dialect with Mr Joel, leaving Hamish bemused.

'The authorities think I store Turkish delights here! Can they not see that I have no free spaces in my cold-store for men-meat? I have space only for animal-flesh. And what is all this doing for my business?'

'But Mr Joel, they'll pay you? For the damage?'

'Reparations! For broken hinges and much lost flesh. So what compensation for lost customers?' He picked up a cloth and made as if to wipe a shelf but

8

instead wiped his forehead. Then, from a glass jar which had not been shattered, he fished out a gherkin, brown and warty as a toad. He presented it to Hamish.

'For you. For your friendly face in time of despair. Youth is the hope for the future.'

With the minty taste of toothpaste still in his mouth, mingling now with the acid of shock, Hamish couldn't even pretend to eat the gherkin. 'Bit early for a snack. I'll save it for later. Thank you.'

'Bitte schön.'

Hamish picked up a paper napkin from the pile which used to sit neatly beside the gherkin jar but now lay scattered on the floor. He folded the gherkin into it and slid it into his pocket to join the slice of blutwurst from last week.

Mr Joel took a clean apron from a plastic pack and tied it on. 'So off you canter now, young man, to your teachers to become wise and save the sad world for me.'

Hamish hurried to his bus stop with a thundering heart. He stood in the queue. As the crowded bus approached, he realized that his white shirt and grey trousers were splattered with crimson as though he had been involved in a violent stabbing incident. Nobody drew attention to the blood–stains. They were scrabbling to maintain their places in the surge to board the bus. Hamish stepped back, buttoned his blazer as if to keep out the cold, turned and walked home to change. He took the long way so he wouldn't have to pass Paragon Parade again.

Ms Florence's
Demographic Elucidation

He eventually reached school in time for mid-morning break. He had missed the deadline for handing in workbooks. So he took them round to the staffroom. A stranger answered his tap on the door and knew nothing of Hamish's special disability exemptions. Hamish tried to force his tip-top homework through the open crack. The supply teacher refused to accept it.

'Do you know what time it is?' said the temporary. 'Unorthodox delivery no longer viable. You'll have to put it in the relevant teacher's pigeonhole for Monday.'

'But that's not fair. It has to be in by today or it won't get marked. I've been off sick.'

'Tough. So's half the staff. That's why I'm here.'

'I was caught in a police raid.'

'That's your lookout.'

Hamish was moody for the rest of the day. Was it the fault of the Turks? And if so, who were they?

The first lesson after break was Geography. It wasn't about foreign countries. It was about demography.

'Individuals with bright, enquiring minds will always want to know where their roots lie,' said Ms Florence who wore a pink rabbits'-wool sweater which made her appear softer than she was.

Hamish felt no attachment to anywhere, least of all to Scotland, which he recalled as damp and full of midges even though Douglas, his father, spoke of Scotland as if it were a paradise. Did enthusiasm for one's roots develop only as one grew up? If Hamish belonged anywhere, he supposed it was to London even though neither of his parents was from here.

Ms Florence's teaching method was inflexible. The class was supposed to take down in note-form everything she said.

'Pay attention, everybody. There's a lot to get through,' she began each class, wasting little time on chatty civilities such as Good morning, isn't it a lovely day?

London, as it used to be, does not exist any more. It has grown so large it has become a distorted fusion of a place which has to be called Greater London. The number of people living in this Greater London is seven million, two hundred and eighty-five thousand, and rising. Each year another twenty thousand, according to statistics, arrive, and quite a few more than that join the hurly-burly unofficially and so avoiding the bureaucratic head-count. (Ms Florence did not know how many and seemed irritated with Hamish for asking. 'If you keep on interrupting we're never going to get to the end before the buzzer,' she said. 'You can all ask your questions when I've finished giving you the data.')

The density of people is four thousand four hundred per square mile. (Hamish experienced this concentration of humanity morning and evening when getting on the bus, and also in the school dinner-line. Burly boys who did kick-boxing instead of homework and didn't have breathing problems elbowed him out of the way.) Greater London consists of thirty-three boroughs. In some boroughs, ethnic minority communities currently account for over one-third of the population. This figure is rising. Too many people are trying to live in too small an area of land, a remorseless drift from rural to urban which is not restricted to Great Britain.

Hamish listened and scribbled facts till his fingers ached. He planned how to complete the demography homework assignment in a way that would please Ms Florence. He would bring in a comparison between the high population density, at four thousand four hundred people per square mile, of Great Britain, with the lower density of another European country, say France, at two hundred and eighty five persons per square mile. Except of course the French would be measuring in square kilometres.

Hamish always completed his homework, even when sick. Indeed, being a sickly person enabled him to pay greater attention to writing up notes into meaningful sentences than the average school-attender. He always got good marks. Was that why nobody liked him?

Those people who cannot be contained within Greater London, Ms Florence continued, inhabit the adjoining regions known as the Home Counties. Middlesex, Surrey, Kent, Essex, Hertfordshire, Buckinghamshire and Berkshire. (Hamish reflected how 'Home Counties' made them sound cosy and reliable. He suspected that, like Ms Florence's fluffy sweater, this impression was false and that unhomely things could occur there as easily as anywhere.)

From Ms Florence, Hamish learned that there are fewer ethnic minority groups in the Home Counties than in Greater London, except around the Kentish ports of Dover and Folkestone where they arrive, hidden in container lorries or clinging to the undersides of trains. They disperse, unnoticed, towards the overcrowded conurbations. In the coming decade, the population increase of Great Britain would be caused not by a rise in live births but by the unstoppable flood of economic immigrants.

Hamish raised his hand. 'Miss!' he said. 'Please, miss.' The incident of the search for Turks in the cold-store, even though none had been found, suddenly made sense. And it was relevant to the topic. He wanted to share the information with the rest of the class. But Ms Florence did not like being interrupted.

'Not now, Hamish. Afterwards,' she said.

Several people sniggered.

Family Tree

Hamish knew little about Anne-Marie's roots beyond that she spoke four languages and came from a village that used to be part of Germany, then turned into France, then back to Germany, then back to France. Her grandparents had originated from opposite sides of a changing national border.

'Sounds a messy carfuffle,' Hamish said. 'How can one country become another? It doesn't make sense.'

'Ah, 'Amish.' The H always fell off the front of his name when his mother said it. 'I can't hexplain now.' She repositioned the dropped Hs into other words. 'When you learn some more 'istory you will hunderstand.'

Hamish knew more about his father's roots, for Douglas liked to reminisce about isles and lochs, castles and crofts, kilts and customs. To be born north of the border made a man more wholesome than to be born anywhere else. A Scot was stronger, more honourable, more adaptable, and more eident, which meant diligent and industrious and was one of Douglas's favourite virtues. Scotland had produced the world's greatest engineers, sailors, rugby players, inventors. Hamish supposed that it was due to being the son of an eident Scot that he always got his homework done. Scots were also lyrical in spirit, had poetry in their souls. (Hamish did not think he'd inherited this trait.)

'The finest writers of the last three centuries have all been Scots. A ballad sung by a Scottish baritone at dusk overlooking the water is one of the most stirring sounds of all time.'

Hamish found his father's enthusiasm perplexing. 'If Scotland's nirvana, why do we live here and not back there?'

'We Scots,' said Douglas, 'are braw roamers, travellers, explorers. Think of Robert Louis Stevenson, all the way to the South Sea Isles he went.'

While Douglas delivered his discourse on Caledonian wonders, Anne-Marie bent her head lower over her book. She didn't take sides.

Douglas said, 'Where the English are concerned, the Scots and the French have always been close partners. On account of the Auld Alliance.'

'What?'

Douglas was fykie over correct speech. 'Wot, wot,

wot! If you followed your own path, I dare say you would soon be footering with innit and wassit too? A crude tongue denies language its full flowering. I take your question to be, What is the Auld Alliance?'

Hamish wished he hadn't asked. Douglas's explanation was long-winded, yet eager, as though the Franco-Scottish coalition against their common enemy had happened last week rather than seven hundred years ago.

Why did Hamish so distrust his father's nationalist tendencies? One was supposed to honour one's father, perhaps even love him. Why couldn't he feel mildly fond of him?

Hamish probably loved Anne-Marie, though he couldn't be sure. Even the heir to the throne of England, Scotland, Wales and Northern Ireland admitted on telly that he didn't know what love was. And Hamish had nothing to compare his feeling for Anne-Marie with. No brothers or sisters, no pets because of the breathing problem. There was Heather, the grandmother, in her croft beside the loch. But you can't feel affection for someone you've only visited twice.

'Maman,' he asked Anne-Marie. 'Am I adopted?'

'Don't be so foolish, 'Amish!' she said.

'Really?'

' 'Eavens above. *I* was the one 'oo push you out. *I* am the woman 'oo know.'

'Okay. Just wondered, that's all.' He closed the topic before she talked childbirth. They'd already done that stuff in PSHE.

He hungered for the future time when he would get away. But how was it ever going to be possible when he relied on Anne-Marie each time he had one of his attacks? No one else would be able to judge it right, that fine line between calmly administering the drug and hoping the crisis would pass, and knowing when to dial for the paramedics to rush in and shove the oxygen tubes up his nostrils.

'Maman?'

She glanced up from her book. 'Yes, 'Amish my dear.'

'Can asthmatics become explorers?' If Robert Louis Stevenson could reach the South Sea Islands despite tuberculosis, was there a chance that Hamish and his asthma could move away from London and its high population density?

' 'Amish! Hall sees funny questions! What 'as got hinto you now?'

Natural restlessness and the desire to be apart from their family comes to everyone as they start to realize that the world is broader than they'd assumed when they first viewed the four sides of their cots.

★ ★ ★

Some evenings, Douglas had to work later than others. To Hamish this was a relief, a time of respite. One evening, when Douglas still wasn't home by eight o'clock, Hamish put a pizza in the microwave. After six minutes, he took it out. He sliced it in half, put each of the halves on to a plate, gave one to Anne-Marie who went on writing notes in the margin of her book, and ate the other himself while he checked his school time-table for the following day. Then he said goodnight, kissing Anne-Marie on both cheeks as he always did. She returned the double-cheek kiss, which he found less extraordinary than the way she pronounced certain words. He went along the corridor to his room. He closed his bedroom door.

He got out his collection of flags of the nations. There was not a lot he could do with them, his room being too small to display more than six at a time. He could probably rearrange them into some special order in the box, say alphabetical, or in order of the chronological date in which each country had gained its independence from the colonial power. It had never been his idea to collect flags. It was the hospital occupational therapist who had suggested to Anne-Marie that Hamish needed an absorbing home hobby since he could not get involved in vigorous sport.

Hamish considered how, when he eventually managed to leave home, which would not happen till he went to university, he would leave behind the flag collection.

When he heard the rap at the front door, he switched out the light and lay down for sleep without questioning why Douglas would not let himself in with his own front-door key.

Douglas had not come home. The fervent Scot deserted the family before Hamish had his own chance to, and in a far from pleasant manner. The stushie at the station in the rush-hour was the start of many adjustments to Hamish's home life.

Douglas and the
Police Officers

The end was brutal and seemingly futile. He was returning home from the office. The platform was crowded, as usual for that time of day. There was scarcely space for the crush of commuters awaiting the train. As several witnesses pointed out afterwards, there is always some shoving and elbowing. It is inevitable when tired workers face an uncomfortable journey before they can put their feet up. It is natural to be irritated when one's tiny personal space is invaded by a sharp-cornered briefcase, an umbrella point, a thoughtlessly-carried backpack.

Tucked under Douglas's arm was an evening paper though there was not yet space in which to unfold it. Several rail users admitted that, on the day in question, they had been aware of being pushed closer than usual towards the edge of the platform. Some had tried to move back, even at the risk of not being able to board the next train and having to wait for the one after. By taking the later train, they'd be assured of a seat but would reach home so late that it would hardly seem worth the effort, given that they'd have to set out again less then eleven hours on. In the station that evening, the commuters were like lab rats crammed into too small a cage. Many felt that their endurance was being stretched beyond reasonable limits.

Douglas, however, was standing his ground, maintaining his position in the mass of shoulder-to-shoulder strangers when a knife was thrust into his side. It went through his dark blue suit, through his white shirt, between two of his lower ribs. It punctured his lung. Douglas was seen to stagger, clutching his chest. The crowd was so dense that for a moment it held him. But as he slumped forward, taking on more personal space than a man was entitled to, the crowd withdrew involuntarily. Several bystanders supposed it was a traveller having a heart attack. When Douglas toppled off the edge of the platform and on to the line minutes before the train was due to enter the station, several more believed they were witnessing a suicide. Nobody knew about the knife till later.

The newspaper which had been tucked under Douglas's arm, carried a report of medical research showing how peak-time travellers face greater anxiety levels than fighter pilots or riot police. Their heart-rates rise to a high of 145bpm which causes spontaneous retreat into a light hypnotic trance as a defence mechanism.

The transport police arrived first, then the paramedics. The station would have to be evacuated, the line closed. Nobody would reach their home at a reasonable time.

The detective inspector in charge of the case observed, 'It seems there was neither rhyme nor reason for this senseless attack. It appears that the deceased did not know the assailant. So far as we know, the accused had not set eyes on the victim before that fateful evening. It would seem to have been random.'

Had the assailant not started to struggle against the flow of commuters still swarming down the steps towards the platform, there might have been a clean getaway. As it was, a quick escape was prevented by the density of the crowd, at first unwittingly, then deliberately. Two members of the public, seeing Douglas fall, thought that the person beside him had tried to push him onto the line. While most travellers were wearing dark suits and ties, the murderer was easy to pick out, in a hooded sweatshirt and jogging pants.

Several people later gave statements to the effect that they'd definitely noticed the threatening look in his dark eyes and had known that he was a villain. Such testaments had to be discounted. The accused was a woman. Her curly hair had been hidden under the hood of her sweatshirt. If there had been some strange look in her eye, it was that of madness rather than badness, psychosis rather than iniquity.

Hamish and Anne-Marie knew nothing of all this, only that Douglas hadn't come home at his usual time. Hamish was under his hypoallergenic duvet with his head on his allergy-free pillow by the time the two police officers, one male, one female, were let into the flat.

Anne-Marie, in her dressing-gown, was clutching her book on medieval Provençal husbandry when the woman officer spoke her well-rehearsed words.

'Will you sit down please? I am afraid we have some bad news.'

Bereavement

He found himself, briefly, at the centre of the drama. He felt distinctly uncomfortable about this. Moreover, Anne-Marie's frequent tears were wearing.

'I never really got on with him anyway,' he muttered, in a misjudged attempt to find something, anything, positive about the situation. This made her cry some more. So he tried to correct himself. If there were times when lying to adults was acceptable, even commendable, this was one of them. 'I don't really mean that. I mean, like I feel I'd hardly got to know him properly. He was out at work so much. That's what I mean.'

She sighed. ' 'Ee was halways a caring father to you,' she said, a curious statement in Hamish's view. Didn't fathers always care for their sons? The more unsettling part was that Hamish had had so few affectionate feelings for Douglas. If only he had, he might now be able to summon up a greater sense of sadness and loss.

But perhaps love, like the awareness of roots, only came with age?

For the time being, he told himself firmly, they must both accept that what had happened had happened and must carry on as best they could.

His raincoat was still hanging in the passageway. Nothing in the flat had been changed except that it was quieter without him. His voice with the faintly accented lilt was no longer telling Hamish what to do, how to speak properly, how to behave like a true and manly Scot. Yet in that stillness, Hamish sometimes had an awareness that Douglas was about to come back, to stride in, start haranguing him over some small detail that summed up Hamish's total failure as a human being.

So you'll be taking care of your mother, he heard Douglas say. And he felt angry. Of course he'd be taking care of Anne-Marie, though he had no idea what they'd live on. Anne-Marie's job at the library was only part-time. He was about to ask her if she'd thought of requesting a full-time position but decided better of it and went and made fried eggs on toast for them both instead.

Hamish's dissimilarity from other boys was more marked than ever. Alone in his sad uniqueness, his asthma attacks increased in frequency and severity.

'Please 'Amish, don't *do* this to me!' Anne-Marie pleaded late at night as he lay gasping for air to pass down the tightened airways.

All he could do in reply was roll his eyes balefully. She fussed with the steam kettle and the inhaler and the tablets and wondered whether the situation warranted the 999. 'You know I couldn't bear to lose you too.'

There were more visits to the health centre, the chest clinic, the family trauma unit, the paediatric psychologist.

'Are you under a lot of stress, would you say?' the psychologist asked Hamish.

Hamish shrugged. 'Isn't everybody? Stress is all around us. In urban areas the population density is greater than it has ever been in any previous era.'

Hamish read the newspaper reports which suggested that Douglas's killer had been provoked to such violence by nervous anxiety induced by venturing into the confusing, scurrying real world after the seclusion of a hospital ward. That the patient was out at all was due to the carelessness of the hospital orderlies who were supposed to keep a close watch on all their charges. But due to hospital overcrowding, the orderlies, too, were under constant pressure. They failed to notice when one patient stopped taking the prescribed anti-psychotic Chlorpromazine. They did not notice when one patient went wandering beyond the hospital boundary.

After arrest, the killer was placed under observation, and then, according to the report that Hamish was reading, was sectioned under the Mental Health Act. This sounded like being cut up into appropriate joints as Mr Joel did with his sides of lamb. But Hamish realized it couldn't really mean that for the report went on to say how the patient had been eventually returned to hospital, and was now contained in a locked ward.

'If our mental hospitals continue to be filled beyond their capacity, these unfortunate things will happen,' said the physician superintendent. 'This sector of the health services has long been under funded. And those who devote their lives to this important work need greater respect.'

Hamish did not realize, until he saw a picture of the lunatic killer, that she was a woman and that she was black.

Ahmed's Thirst
for Learning

Hamish thought he was not as other boys. He was wrong. Shocking things could happen to other children too. Far away to the south, in a country of which Hamish knew nothing except the colours and design of its national flag (under the previous non-elected regime), another boy was getting ready to go to school. He didn't know it would be for the last time. He wanted to be able to go to school. He had to learn more about the many wonders of the world, about the Blue Mosque with its doors inlaid with ivory, shell, mother-of-pearl, built in Istanbul for Sultan Ahmet I, about the Pyramids of the Pharaohs, about the Alhambra Palace in Grenada, and about General Napoleon Bonaparte's Arc de Triomphe in France. He did not expect, as a poor country boy, ever to visit these sites, but he wanted to understand them and the reasons behind their creation.

He was awake before the sun. For breakfast he ate flat bread with dried fish and drank a glass of tea sweetened with a spoonful of condensed milk. He pulled on his jacket and his woolly cap for at this hour of the morning it was chilly. He set out. Long ago, according to his elder brothers, there used to be a bus. No longer. Ahmed could scarcely even remember how things used to be before the change of leadership.

It was a walk of eleven kilometres. If only he could have biked. While Usman, his next eldest brother, was still attending school, they'd ridden together, with Ahmed balanced on the crossbar. As soon as Usman was half strong enough to do a man's work, his days of education were over. He had taken the bicycle with him when he left home to look for work.

The sun came up greyish-pink, paled by the sand-dust hanging in the air. The wind they called the harmattan swept it off the desert. It was a dry wind which lowered the humidity, creating hot days and cool nights. Every wind had its own name. Ahmed only knew those of his own area. One day he would learn about all the winds of the world. One day, he would know so much about everything that he would pass his matriculation into high school. He was already the first person in his family to go beyond Grade 4. His mother could not read. His father only scarcely. Every single day in school counted. He would become the first person in his village to qualify as a teacher. With the help of men like Monsieur Bruno, he would change the world, not the entire world, but this small part of it. He knew of his father's struggle to support the family. With an education and a profession Ahmed would be able to help his parents and himself to a better future.

He followed the dirt road between the olive groves. The trees hadn't been tended for many seasons. Men didn't work the land. They went to the phosphates factory instead. Olives shrivelled on the branches and dropped into the dusty weeds beneath. There was a shorter route to school. But it was safer to stay with the main track. You never knew who you might meet if you strayed too far. Moreover, once you'd left the road, you'd miss your chance of a lift with a passing vehicle. Arriving at school early was good. There was always something to do, whether setting out the pupils' wooden benches, washing the schoolroom floor with the bucket and mop, filling the water-filter from the hydrant in the street. There hadn't been a caretaker to see to these tasks for a long while, not since before the change of regime.

He heard an engine in the distance. He turned to welcome the cloud of dust as it drew nearer. When the driver saw him, he would stop. Even if it was a truck laden high with wood or rocks or livestock or chemical fertilizer, the driver would let him climb up and hang on where he could. The red dust swelled. The vehicle approached at surprising speed considering the terrain. It was a Citroën DS, low-slung, its hydraulic suspension making it capable of bounding over the fissures and pot-holes. The pink sun glinted off the windscreen so he couldn't see if the car was full. But they would surely give him a lift however many passengers were already packed in.

Today would be an early arrival at school. He would have time to sweep out the yard as well as seeing to the classroom. Then Monsieur Bruno might spare a few moments to give him extra help with his calcul.

Ahmed was confused by the DS. Instead of slowing, it was accelerating. How could the driver fail to notice him when he was the only figure on this long straight stretch? Ahmed jumped backwards and down into the storm-drain just in time. The black tyres of the Citroën passed less than a hand's stretch from where he'd been standing, throwing up a vicious spray of sand. It was almost as though the driver had been deliberately aiming for him. Was he trying to scare him?

He was not angry and he was not surprised. Many strange things were said to be happening. His mother assured him that they were only rumours, that it was not in anybody's interest to listen to or to repeat rumours.

He climbed out of the ditch, brushed himself down. Was it wise to continue? Had the driver been giving him some kind of warning? Might it be safer to turn back, even though he'd risk his mother's displeasure and lose a day's learning?

He watched the car's swirl of dust disappear into the distance. This road had turned out to be just as dangerous as the short-cut, so he might as well take that route. He scrambled through the thorn-hedge into the abandoned olive-grove and hurried on his way, wishing one of his elder brothers was here to protect him but they had long since followed their father in search of work. Ahmed missed them, his father too, who gave his blessing to Ahmed's enthusiasm for study. 'I didn't have this opportunity,' his father had said. 'You do. So hold it with your two hands.'

Hamish and Watkins

Having a father whose picture (an old one taken long before the murder) had been in all the newspapers where it could be seen by other pupils, made Hamish feel conspicuous. And if that was bad, Ms Florence managed to make it worse by nominating Timothy Watkins to be Hamish's buddy. Watkins was otherwise known as Dim Tim or sometimes Dim Sum.

Ms Florence came upon Hamish lurking in the cloakroom designing flags in his Maths book instead of being outside in the fresh air. 'You're a bit of a loner, aren't you Hamish?' she observed.

'Yes, Miss, I suppose so.' If that was what she'd set her heart on him being, there was nothing he could do to alter her perception. It was her job to alter his view of things, not the other way round. 'It's because of my condition. I'm not supposed to breathe air when it's cold.'

'Quite apart from that. You're a curious young fellow,' she went on. 'You *could* have a lot going for you.' She smiled at him with her soft rabbit smile which Hamish knew to be false. A wolf in rabbit's clothing. When she continued to smile, Hamish was momentarily alarmed that she was going to ruffle his hair like the woman from the launderette had when she'd heard about the stabbing. But Ms Florence's deportment was quite correct. She kept her hands to herself. 'Why don't you mix with other boys? It would be better than this moping.'

'Sure,' said Hamish. 'I'll give it a try when I'm not so busy. Right now, I've got a lot of grieving to get through.' This was an expression he'd overheard the policewoman use when speaking to Anne-Marie. He'd decided to save it up for future use.

'Yes of course,' said Ms Florence. 'We all know it has been difficult for you recently. However, I think the time to mix with others is not later, but now. If you don't start soon, you'll find it gets harder. Everybody needs someone to rely on. Since you don't appear to have a special close friend within the school, I've nominated Timothy to be your buddy for the rest of this term.'

People only had to have a buddy if there was something profoundly wrong with them, like they were deaf or albino or in a wheelchair (and there was only one of each of those in the whole school. That meant three people with buddies. Now four).

'You'll find you have lots in common.'

How could a high-achiever like himself have anything in common with an under-achiever like Dim Sum? For a start, Hamish knew that Watkins was adopted. This knowledge made him uncomfortable though he didn't understand why.

Two more bad things were to happen that day, which was precisely what the woman from the launderette had predicted. After telling Hamish what a shame it was about his dad, she'd added, 'And you better watch your back, laddie! Trouble always comes in threes!'

The conscription of Watkins as Hamish's buddy proved to be no protection. The next bad thing was during the mid-morning lesson-break when pupils and staff scurry between classrooms. One has to watch one's back. And one's front. And specially one's ears, since older boys liked to whack smaller boys' ears from behind with a ruler. They called it slicing the bacon.

Hamish thought how like chickens people were. Put them together in a confined space and they start ripping out each other's neck feathers. Chickens are probably cannibalistic. When push comes to shove they'd eat each other. (If rats didn't get there first.)

A crowded corridor is no place for a person with a breathing problem. As Hamish struggled through the rushing chicken-stream from Maths to Geography he was pick-pocketed. He discovered the theft during Geography.

Ms Florence threw up on to the plasma screen the west-to-east cross-section of the lower and upper carboniferous rocks of the North Pennines. She said, 'Basalt is an igneous rock, most commonly formed as a lava flow at the ground surface.'

Hamish reached into his blazer breast-pocket for his pen to write this down. His pen was absent. Everything had gone. Bus pass. Library card. Mobile. Pencil case. Gold-nib free-flow Mont Blanc fountain pen (birthday gift from Anne-Marie though she had pretended it was from Douglas). Front door key. Locker key. (On separate fobs in separate pockets.)

How had the thieving rat managed to slide his slimy mitt into four different pockets about Hamish's person without him noticing? Or had it been four separate rats operating as a team?

Hamish became ignited. Rage and humiliation flowed like hot lava.

'So, recent basaltic lava flows create plains with a characteristically rough, dark surface. Certain distinctive features can also be identified in the relief.'

Hamish had no time for all that. It was highly disturbing to be victim of an unknown person who might be laughing about him even at this minute. He scanned the room but nobody caught his searching eye. He reached into his bag for his inhaler. At least the thief hadn't taken that. He applied the inhaler to his mouth for two quick puffs. It was a useful decoy. No teacher could prohibit a pupil from using prescribed medication.

Usman was most likely the culprit. He had contempt for anyone who was not like himself, and a reputation for nicking things, then selling them back to you. Or what about Morris? He was thick, and the lackey of Usman. Stupid people often thieved to gain themselves credibility. Or Bennett? Or Akri? Every one of them had ridiculed Hamish on at least one occasion.

The quickest way to get over being demeaned was to humiliate someone else. But who? And on what grounds?

'And note the colouring of the basalt, which can be black, bluish or a leaden grey.'

Hamish had no pen with which to note this down. He leaned over to Watkins, the requisitioned buddy. 'Hey, Dim Sum,' he whispered.

Watkins blinked. 'Er what?'

Hamish said, 'Mr and Mrs Watkins aren't your real parents, are they?'

Watkins whispered, 'Yes. As real as can be because they *chose* me,' then added in a breathy rush, 'Don't know where from. Think I might be a bit Spanish. My hair's dark enough. I'd like to be descended from a Spanish pirate.'

'Idiot! There aren't pirates any more.'

'Or at least some kind of seafarer, and to sail the seven seas.'

What must it be like, Hamish wondered, to have no roots at all, not even the faraway roots of Scotland? He said, 'It's important to know your true origins. You heard Ms Florence.'

Watkins shook his head. 'No. It's good this way. Then I can imagine whatever I want. I've told Mum that's what I do. She doesn't mind. She likes me as I am. So do I.'

Hamish thought, How *could* Watkins like himself? 'Any reasonable person in your situation would want to find out.' He glanced at Watkins's open workbook, a mess of splodges, crossings-out. What kind of parents would choose a person who didn't even know how to keep a tidy page? He felt a surge of bitter jealousy. Why should Dim Tim have been chosen whereas he had not? At every turn, life was less than fair. 'Be a pal. Lend us a pen. Mine's been half-inched.'

Without a second's hesitation, Watkins handed over the fibre-tip pen lying beside the workbook, in readiness for him to make more inky chaos on the page. It had TIMOTHY WATKINS stamped on in gold letters so that even though he must have been aware that everybody thought of him as Dim Tim or Dim Sum, Watkins's identity remained secure.

The pen was nothing like a gold-nibbed Mont Blanc. The fibre-tip had been so distorted by Watkins's clammy hold that it was like writing with a twig. If Hamish got his own pen back he'd return Watkins's. Then again, he might not. He owed Watkins nothing. It hadn't been his idea to ask Watkins to look after him.

During lunch-break, Hamish was seized by an acute attack. Asthma is unpredictable. The bronchial tubes tighten suddenly. The chest cavity goes into spasm. The lungs collapse in on themselves.

He'd been put through weeks of testing at the clinic. Nobody claimed to know definitively the cause. One specialist suggested a food allergy. Another said there was an emotional trigger. Hamish was given a sheet of relaxation techniques. If the latest expert was right, then this sudden constriction of the bronchial passages, the swelling of their linings which led to this terrifying sensation of suffocation, was caused by Hamish's own inner anger.

Two younger boys passed Hamish in the doorway and mimicked the rasping death rattle coming from his throat.

'Here he goes again! The whimpering wheezer!'

The new supply teacher came by. He thought Hamish was bluffing but when he saw him grapple to get the cap off the aerosol inhaler he guided Hamish to the medical room. Hamish passed the afternoon sitting by the radiator staring out of the grilled window like a prisoner.

At the end of the day, although Hamish's breathing was under control, he was still seething at the inconvenience caused to his well-being by the morning's theft. Travel-cardless, he was going to have to sneak his way on to the bus via the exit door without the driver spotting him on the CCTV screen.

Hamish's asthma was an undesirable but banal aspect of daily life so did not count as the day's third bad thing. This third bad thing was finding that Anne-Marie was not yet home.

He had no key. He had to sit on the steps, waiting. He did his homework with Watkins's scratchy pen until the light in the stairwell grew too dim. When she finally returned, she was accompanied by two police officers. She looked as though she'd been crying. He hated it when she cried. He thought she'd given it up.

Ahmed and
the Militia

Ahmed knew something was wrong before he reached the compound. There were no other pupils chattering like noisy birds. He ran the last stretch to the railings. There was no smiling Monsieur Bruno at the gate to welcome them in. The gate was locked with a chain and padlock.

Perhaps Monsieur Bruno had overslept? It had happened before, only once, when he had been sick with fever. Monsieur Bruno had a single-roomed lodge within the compound, just behind the classroom. Ahmed shouted out polite morning greetings to his teacher as loudly as he could in the hope of waking him if he were asleep. Then he saw how the glass of several of the windows was shattered and that parts of the mud wall above those windows was smoke-blackened. The gates had been secured with the chain from the outside. If anybody was still inside the compound they must have been locked in by someone else. Ahmed would rather believe that the school was deserted and that Monsieur Bruno had gone away.

Who could Ahmed go to for information? The nearest houses had their shutters closed. A car nosed out of an alleyway and moved towards him. It was that Citroën DS again. This time the windows were down. He could see three men squashed in the front, more sitting behind. They were armed. People had a right to protect themselves if they could afford to. What was unusual was that two of the men had their weapons resting on the window edge and pointed them at Ahmed as the saloon sidled up alongside him.

Ahmed had not been so close to the wrong end of a weapon before. He gave the morning greeting to the driver who didn't return it but growled an order.

'Get out of here. You don't want trouble.'

The man next to him confirmed the message with a gesture of his gun. Then the car drove off and Ahmed did as he'd been told. He headed for home keeping as low to the ground as a slinking hyena, darting from one thicket to the next, afraid and guilty, though he knew he had done nothing wrong.

He knew that his plan to become a respected teacher had never been anything but a foolish daydream.

Anne-Marie and the
Boy Joy-riders

After the two police officers who drove her home had taken a written statement from Anne-Marie, they explained how to cancel stolen bank cards. Then they arranged for a locksmith to come and change the lock on the front door.

'While we're at it, we might as well check your window catches,' one said cheerily. 'Better safe than sorry, eh?'

Then they went away.

Hamish made sliced cheese on toast for Anne-Marie and himself. While they waited for the locksmith to turn up, Anne-Marie told Hamish again what had happened. He'd already heard it once when she was telling the police, going slowly because they'd found her hard to follow. This time, she garbled rapidly, occasionally becoming upset and so lapsing into French without realizing it.

Hamish conceded that Anne-Marie's unpleasant incident of the day was worse than his own. And, since the front-door lock had got to be changed, it didn't matter any more about his own key. As far as he could gather, this was what had happened to her:

She was driving home from the library when a red light on the dashboard started blinking. At first, she took no notice. It was nothing to do with her. She didn't understand car engines. Douglas always saw to things like that. But she understood it to be the fuel-gauge warning light. On empty. 'But 'ow can you tell?' she said, shrugging her shoulders hopelessly.

It went on blinking. She knew that if the car ran out of fuel on the dual carriageway as darkness fell, she'd be in trouble. She lessened her speed which, apparently, reduced fuel consumption. She'd seen it on the television when Hamish had been watching *Top Gear*. ' 'Eavens know, 'Amish!' she had exclaimed at the time. 'Why you watch these things! It is many years before you har driving my car!'

'Was waiting for that cookery programme,' Hamish had replied.

When Anne-Marie saw the yellow glow of the filling station ahead she felt such joy. But she had to queue for a free pump. At last it was her turn. She got out and went to unlock the petrol cover. She wished these places weren't self-service. In the village where she grew up there was always somebody to do it for you, usually the son of the mechanic. She wrestled to fit the key into the petrol cap. Why did they have to put locks on these things? Nobody would be stupid enough to try to steal petrol!

The cap seemed jammed. Or else she hadn't the knack. She looked round for another customer who would help her. The forecourt was empty. The only other human was at the till inside the glass-fronted shop. She scurried over the greasy Tarmac to ask him for help. But the entrance door was closed. She banged on it. The man beckoned to her to come round to the grilled window at the front.

'I cannot get the hat open,' she shouted through the glass. 'You must come and do 'im for me.'

He had a black beard and dark eyes. She didn't trust him but there was no one else to ask. 'Sorry ma'am,' he replied without needing to shout for the window was miked. 'Can't leave the till unattended.'

'So what ham I to do?' Anne-Marie asked.

'How far do you have to go? Perhaps you've enough to see you home?'

'Why won't you 'elp me?' Anne-Marie pleaded. 'You are not from 'ere, are you? You'll learn that in this place we all try to 'elp each other.'

She walked back to the car, angry. Why were people in this country always so unwilling to help? As she opened the driver's door, she was grabbed from inside by a big boy with a beanie cap low over his forehead. He had been crouching down in the passenger seat, waiting for her to come back. She saw him as soon as she opened the door.

' 'Oo hare you? What hare you doing inside my car?'

He pulled her in and shoved her roughly over the seat-backs into the rear.

'You 'ave no right!' she protested.

'Get down. Lie down!' he ordered. He didn't sound very mature. His voice was high.

Another boy scrambled into the driving seat. He, too, seemed slight and young. She didn't feel afraid and was too astonished to shout. What use would that have been with such an impassive attendant, safely locked in with his till behind the unbreakable glass?

They found Anne-Marie's bag on the floor under the driver's seat and rifled through her things. She didn't know if they had a gun.

They didn't find what they were looking for.

'Kiss. Give us the kiss!'

'Kiss?' Anne-Marie echoed, with a sinking realization that this was a worse situation than she'd first thought.

'Keys, you deaf bint!'

'She's foreign,' said the first of the boys and grabbed the keys from Anne-Marie's tight fist. 'And your purse. Are you stupid too?'

The other boy said, 'You got to talk to them in their own language. Où est votre sac? That's what you have to say. Le-sac-de-ma-tante-est-dans-le— Don't know how it goes after that.'

'Shut up!' said the first boy to his companion and threw a jacket over Anne-Marie's head. 'And you, don't move! One move and that's it! Fini. Finito. Capishez?'

Anne-Marie heard the engine start and stall and start again. She felt the car jerk forward. The boy-driver might have known two French phrases but he didn't know how to change gear. After five minutes of travelling noisily and bumpily along in bottom gear, they juddered to an unexpected halt. The doors were opened. The jacket was pulled off her head. She was pushed on to the grass. Her car lurched off without headlights like a kangaroo at dusk. She was on her own in a lay-by, without her bag, her jacket, her keys, her attaché case with the notes she'd made during her lunch-hour in the library about the popes of Avignon. Her retreat into fourteenth-century France was the only interest that had been keeping her afloat during the past dark weeks. She trudged back along the dual carriageway towards the filling station. She could see the glow hanging like an oasis in the damp black air. Like a mirage, it was further than she thought. It took her forty minutes to reach. Then the police arrived quickly.

'The till assistant here says he tried to warn you.'

Anne-Marie said she didn't know, she couldn't remember, but that it was the assistant's fault it had happened in the first place. 'He should 'ave come out and 'elped. I could not hunlock the gasoline capot,' she said. 'If this man had 'elp me sis would 'ave be a different story. 'As 'e never 'ear of the benevolent Samaritan?'

The assistant said, 'They were probably just kids, messing about. You get a lot of it round here. It's the school exclusions causing it. These kiddies don't realize the upset they cause.'

Anne-Marie said sternly, 'Sey are thieves and kidnappers.'

The police officers did their best to calm her, agreed that kidnapping was a serious offence, and then drove her home and forced open her front door.

Anne-Marie, Victim

Hamish reflected on the various accounts of her ordeal. She said she had told the police in her statement that the kidnappers were two big, dark men.

Hamish said, 'Hey, Maman, that's different from what you said before. Why did you tell the police they were big and dark if you only saw one of them?'

'I was hangry. Of course sey were black. What else would they be? Round 'ere what do you expect?'

Hamish thought it was wrong to give inaccurate information to the police. He said, 'They'll go looking for the wrong people!' But would that be any different from looking for Turks in places where there was nothing but cold raw meat?

Anne-Marie said she did not care if the wrong people were arrested. 'I 'ate all sose people 'oo make me feel the stranger. They are the aliens. And I 'ate this country! One day I will get haway from 'ere!'

Hamish had not heard her say this before.

'Of course I 'ate it 'ere! I 'ave hallways 'ated it! But I 'ad nowhere else!'

When Douglas had been alive, he was the one who calmed Anne-Marie when she became distressed. Hamish could shut himself in his room and sort out his flags. But now he had to do the calming. He made her a cup of tea, switched on the heater in her room, then persuaded her to take a relaxing bath.

The car was found not far on from the lay-by where Anne-Marie had been tipped out, abandoned when it ran out of fuel. It was released to Anne-Marie once it had been fingerprinted. Her hand-bag was still under the driver's seat, the attaché case containing the notes she had made on the antics of the priests of medieval Provence lying, untouched, on the back seat.

Hamish and Usman

In front of the school gates, Hamish could see a busy fight, like fireworks at ground level. Normally, he avoided fights, for he knew that he was the one that others most wanted to hit, specially after class marks had been announced and he was top again. It looked as if it was Usman down on the ground, lashing out to defend himself against a ring of attackers. Hamish could only see the back of his head. He was wearing one of those stupid woollen caps his gang all wore. They kept them tucked into their backpacks. They pulled them on as soon as they had a foot outside the school boundary. You were supposed to wear your uniform until you reached your home.

Hamish was certain it was Usman who'd nicked his stuff, though he hadn't yet tried to flog it back. It made Hamish red with anger. How dare he? Usman had come out of nowhere, from some badlands in Africa, the Dark Continent, Douglas said it used to be called, and his family got given a flat and benefits and that made Usman behave as though he had the right to nick things from other people who actually belong here so had a lot greater rights to go on living here peacefully.

There were six or seven older students crowding round the fracas, all girls, each having a go at the defeated body on the ground. No doubt they, too, were victims of Usman's greedy thieving. None of Usman's pals were around to protect him so it seemed safe for Hamish to close in.

They managed to keep him down. He was rounding his back to protect his groin, trying to protect his face with his hands. His arrogant face wasn't worth protecting, Hamish thought, viciously. Hamish stepped forward and aimed a little kick in the ribs. It must have been harder than he meant. The impact hurt his toes. Hamish had never heard a bone crack but that was what it sounded like. What a triumph! He remembered Douglas telling him how the undefeated Scots warrior picked up a severed English head off the field of battle and kicked it, like a football, back across the border into Northumberland.

'Take that, you scum!' Hamish said in a voice which came out smaller and reedier than he'd have liked.

'Okay, enough's enough,' said one of the bystanders, a girl. 'Let's not overdo it. She's got the message.'

They backed off. On the ground, Usman groaned and turned over. Hamish had a shock when he saw the blazer badge. It didn't have the gold bars and white lily pattern against the dark background. It was blue and reddish, from the other secondary school which was all girls.

When the victim staggered to its feet it was definitely not Usman.

Even though Hamish was never normally in fights, he knew the rules. You weren't supposed to hit females because they were weak, their bones were soft, and they didn't know how to fight back. He felt ashamed but only mildly for, he reasoned, he hadn't realized that the girl he'd kicked on her back *was* a girl so it wasn't entirely his fault and if she'd wanted to be treated like a female she shouldn't have been wearing trousers and had such short hair.

The female he knew best was Anne-Marie. He considered her delicately thin wrists, her tissue-paper appearance, her general frailty as if a light breeze might blow her over. He knew that if he actually saw anyone try to hit her he'd definitely want to hit them back. So if, by some chance, he ever encountered that girl again, he'd let her give him a good kick if she wanted to, to even things up.

As he headed for the bus stop, he felt a satisfactory

release from the tensions that had been building up. He felt his maturity coming. He elbowed his way to the front of the queue, past the old grannies with their pushalong shoppers, the young women with their babies in buggies, in order to be first on to get the good seat next to the rear doors where nobody could try and sit near you. He watched the other passengers struggle aboard. Yes, it was a shame about that girl's ribcage but we can all make mistakes – teachers, hospital staff, filling-station assistants, even policemen searching for illegal Turks.

Ahmed and the Lonely Goat

His home was deserted. The neighbours' homes too. It was as if all the women and all their children had left in a hurry. The community centre and two other buildings had been set alight, just like at the school, ineffectually, as if it were a warning, an attempt to destroy human morale more than brick and mud.

The hamlet was silent apart from the whirring of the doves in the trees. The communal grain-store had been ransacked. Even the hens had gone. Ahmed had heard of this kind of thing happening in other places. But not here where, for better for worse, they tried to get along with one another, even more so since the working men had had to leave.

Just one item of domestic livestock had been left behind, a goat tethered to the paling. Whoever had driven everyone away hadn't been bothered with a goat, almost too skinny to eat, and whose milk had dried up. She was straining on the rope for blades of grass beyond her reach.

Ahmed untied her. She would be attacked sooner or later by some predator, a jackal or hyena. Or one of those German dogs that looked like wolves which some people kept. She might at least have her liberty, and even a chance to flee. Better than being devoured while tethered.

On release, the goat showed no inclination to run away, merely trotted a few paces and got busy nibbling at a sheet that had been put out to dry on a thorn bush earlier that day. Ahmed tried to shoo her away. How stupid she was to think that this was a safe place.

Inside his home, he found millet seed scattered over the floor. He scooped up as much of it as he could and poured it carefully into a cotton bag. There was also some spilled maize-flour and two onions. On the shelf was a bottle of coffee essence, and a tin of sardines. He added them to the collection in the bag. He picked up the tin of condensed milk which had been opened at breakfast time. Already it seemed an age ago.

No point in leaving it. The sugar ants had already found their way to it. He flicked off the ones on the outside, and picked out those inside the tin, then poured the thick sweet milk directly into his mouth. He filled a plastic cola bottle with water from the pitcher in the corner which had not been overturned. He took a look round. When would he be back? As a final thought, he took up the knitted blanket from his mother's bed. He was ready to leave. The goat wandered contentedly around the compound. He hesitated by her. Should he take her too? No, she would slow his progress.

He must go to where his father and his next eldest brother worked. He had an uncertain understanding of how far the phosphates factory was. But he knew at any rate to turn towards the west.

Anne-Marie, Hamish
and the Violent Episode

Ever since her husband's death had been reported so enthusiastically in the press, Anne-Marie had given up reading newspapers. That day, however, during her lunch-hour at the library where she worked replacing borrowed books, she skimmed through the local paper to check screening times at the cinema. Hamish and she would benefit from an outing.

A short report caught her eye. She was startled. It concerned her son's school. A shocking event had taken place. Why had he not told her about it? The poor brave boy, protecting his mother from bad news that might upset her.

Pupils Sent Home Following Racist Chants
In an unfortunate incident on Tuesday morning, 40 white pupils from the Eglantine Jebb Secondary School in the western neighbourhood

of the city were forced into their assembly hall by teachers, after they had been chanting racist slogans. They were kept imprisoned until security guards arrived. At the same time, 28 pupils from ethnic minorities, pupils attending the same school, had to be herded into the IT classroom and, for their own safety, kept under lock and key, until police and social workers arrived to resolve the situation.

A spokesperson for the school, Ms Florence, said, 'It was a nasty incident, started by a couple of troublemakers. But it was isolated. And it is all over now.'

Jebb's School, which is situated in a predominantly middle-class, pleasantly green garden-suburb, has been recently targeted by the British National Party which is trying to exploit the issue of immigration and the dispersal of asylum seekers. According to a representative from the Reconciliation and Ethnic Harmony Centre, there have been several accusations of racism, ranging from mild bullying to ferocious physical attacks, mainly directed towards Kurdish, Palestinian, Afghan, Kenyan and Burundi children, and also towards children perceived to be Muslim, Jewish, Seventh Day Adventist, Catholic, Irish, Welsh or Turkish.

Hamish had been swept up into the incident so unexpectedly. And he'd loved every moment of it. He kept going over it in his mind. He'd been minding his own business, wandering along the corridor between the juniors' and the seniors' cloakrooms, when he found himself mixed up in a crowd of older boys who were taunting a group of younger boys. The crowd Hamish was with accepted him as one of them and he felt the warm blanket of companionship. Then, suddenly, it all got super-charged with energy. Hamish's group were being forced back into the assembly hall by three panicking teachers. He felt such a rush of adrenalin. It was like being in that team who'd raided Mr Joel's cold-store, all hyped up, searching out the Turks. Hamish told himself he was acting nobly. He too was seeking out the dark infidels lurking in their midst. More than that, he was exacting revenge for his father's death at the hand of the mad black murderer.

'They had it coming to them!' the chief chanter yelled.

'Had it, had it, had it coming to them, ya ya ya!' the others chorused back, Hamish too though he wasn't entirely sure who had what coming to them.

Then there were vile insults being shouted, words that Hamish knew were bad but he couldn't help himself from shouting those too. It was good humoured enough. There was even some giggling as they were slowly shuffled backwards into the assembly hall by the school secretary wielding a fire-extinguisher.

'Faces to the wall!' she screamed.

'Innocent until proved guilty!' yelled one of the group.

'Every one of you. To the wall. Hands on heads!' The secretary could be scarier than the teaching staff. And when she was, it was exciting as if something of great consequence was happening.

Hamish saw through the assembly hall windows the pathetic group of pupils from the IT room being escorted off the school premises. Around him in the hall, those pupils who were judged by the secretary to be instigators were made to wait for the arrival of the police. It was an arbitrary decision, made by a kangaroo court.

'Free trials for all!' one of the reputed ringleaders called out.

'My dad's a beak!' yelled another and sniggered.

The younger ones, Hamish included, were sent back to their lessons. Hamish hadn't got a lesson to go to. The rest of his class were out on the sports field. He ambled along to the library and read a book about the medieval Children's Crusade which wanted to drive the Moorish Saracens out of the Holy Land.

'I just happened to be there, that's all,' he assured Anne-Marie as she interrogated him about his involvement. 'I didn't tell you before because it wasn't important.'

'Sank God for that,' said Anne-Marie. 'Sank the Lord. I knew you couldn't 'ave been involved. But I worry.'

'You're *always* worried. You don't need to be. It makes you thin.'

'We can't go on like sis,' Anne-Marie said. 'We should go far away, until sings blow in.'

'Blow over,' Hamish corrected her. 'They have blown over. I heard Ms Florence saying so.'

The guilty pupils were suspended. Then they were sentenced by the juvenile court to hours of community service. The BNP was already focusing its activities on another area.

Anne-Marie said, 'I meant for us. Blow over for you and me.'

NORTH
AND
SOUTH

Ahmed and
His Mother

A day's walk took him to the factory where phosphates were processed into fertilizer. It was late. The steel gates were locked. There was no one. He walked the silent streets. He'd expected to find a town bright with life. But it was as dark as his village. He crawled under a stationary truck to shelter but then, in fear that the driver might turn up and crush his legs, he moved on to spend the remainder of the night lying, but not daring to sleep, beside a heap of refuse into which he could burrow if need be. He supposed it was a curfew that kept the people off the streets, though he saw no sight of any militia.

In the morning he returned to the factory. The security guard spoke through the gate, insisting that his relatives were not there. But he would not tell Ahmed when his father or brother had last reported for work. He told Ahmed to go away. Ahmed walked towards the centre of the town.

The dwellings were higher than anything Ahmed had expected and there were no plots for people to grow their vegetables, no acacias to give shade. A while back, he had wanted to explore the world. If this was the world, he did not want to see any more of it.

Each residency had an open concrete stairway with rooms on either side. He walked from block to block climbing the stairs, knocking on the doors, asking anybody who would dare open up if they knew in what neighbourhood the people from his village might be congregating. His father would certainly have advised his mother to stay among people she knew. But people were afraid, even of a boy. Ahmed remembered his father telling him how, when he was young, no person ever closed a door in your face. It was the custom to keep the entrance open to any passerby. If he came into your home, you did not ask where he was from until the third day. If he would not accept a glass of tea or coffee, the host would know that the visitor had a problem that needed solving. It was up to the host to help him find a solution. But that kind of conduct was from a long way back in time.

At last, an old woman opened her door wide enough to say, 'You mean, the wife of the man who was shot? Is that who you want?'

'Shot?' Ahmed felt the steps heave under him. He might have expected his brothers to disobey the militia, to run when asked to stop, to go out when told to remain in. But not his father.

'Not so badly, just in the leg. He was out after the curfew. They ordered him to stand still but he thought he could get away. What can you expect in times like this?' She gave him some garbled directions before closing her door.

Ahmed located his mother three blocks on, lying on a single bed in a stuffy room. She embraced him when she saw him, then wept. Ahmed did not cry. He must behave like a man. He handed over the bag of grain and leftovers he'd brought, and wrapped the knitted blanket round her shoulders as if it were a precious robe. She placed the food in a covered basket under the bed. Then he lay down beside his mother and slept deeply. When he woke she was still there. He understood, though she did not say so, that this narrow iron bed and the space beneath was now their home.

Three other women and their children were living in the same room. The space was divided by curtains looped across on wires.

Ahmed's mother spoke softly, 'Here, I am out of harm's way, so long as I keep quiet. Your father acted imprudently. He could not be persuaded to remain silent about the conditions at work. He believed if he protested he could change things. He has changed nothing for the better, only for the worse. He has ended up injured and without work. He is in a safe house with your uncle. They have made plans and the situation will become much better for all of us.'

The women in the room took turns to cook a meal each evening on a charcoal brazier out in the corridor. Their men came when they could. But they did not come into the curtained room and they did not stay long out on the stairwell. Ahmed was overcome with timidity when he saw his father again. This old man, his cheeks crisscrossed with lines, his beard grizzled, was almost a stranger. How could he have changed so quickly, or had Ahmed misremembered the face?

After the men had gone, Ahmed's mother explained, 'Your uncle knows where there is work. He and your father are going to travel there. They've been delaying the departure till you arrived. You are to go with them. I had faith that you would find me. The journey will be expensive. They have borrowed money. They will repay when you are settled, have secure work and can make us a home. We will only have to be apart for a year, or perhaps two. After that, everything will be good.'

He had survived a day and a night on his own before being reunited with his mother. Their new home was no more than a single bed in the space behind a curtain. Ahmed didn't want to even consider leaving. She insisted. 'No, your father says you will go. In the land of plenty you will be well looked after. Everything is arranged. You go on with your schooling until you are considered old enough to work. It is a wonderful chance for you.'

'Where is it, this special place?'

But she didn't know. She had never travelled further from their village than he had.

Hamish Breathes
a Sigh

The night-time attacks increased. Twice in a week Anne-Marie called the paramedics and he was rushed on the blue light to A & E for the crisis to be brought under control.

'We cannot go on like sis!' Anne-Marie sighed. 'It is killing me with worry.'

Hamish lay beneath the bright strip lighting in his curtained cubicle and nodded. There was nothing he could do but soldier on like a sturdy Scot, just as Douglas used to tell him to.

Douglas's mother, whom Hamish could barely remember, and who hadn't refreshed his memory by attending the funeral, sent a hand-knitted Arran sweater, with a note in quaky handwriting. 'Warm clothing will better the laddie's health.'

'It is that old woman still believe her pitiable daughter-in-law has not understood se British climate!' said Anne-Marie bitterly.

The fatty lanolin in the wool which had been sheared from rugged Scots sheep brought Hamish's skin up in itchy hives.

Other homely remedies were also recommended. Honey in hot water. Graded exercise programmes. Reiki massage. Purging the home of detergent, make-up, shampoo. Anne-Marie's colleagues at the library had as many theories on the causes of asthma as the hospital consultants.

'It's the polluted London air.'

'It's the damp rising from the Thames, mixing with the sulphuric acid.'

'It's the carbon dioxide from all those stupid jeeps.'

'There's more kids with breathing problems here than anywhere else in the world, even Russia where they let all that gas escape.'

'You ought to take the boy somewhere with clean air. What about Scotland? You've got relatives up there, haven't you? It would do you good too. You're looking pale.'

'You owe it to your son to take care of yourself. Try it. See what happens. If it makes no difference, you can come back. You won't have lost anything.'

'We'll still be here waiting for you.'

Ahmed at the
Tower of Babel

The truck drove for a day and a half across unmarked wasteland. They passed a broken jeep, half buried in a dune, and the drying carcass of a camel. They had reached the crossings town. Their driver set them down on an expanse of sand no different from all the rest except that its perimeter was marked out with worn rubber truck-tyres set in the ground and it had a wooden sign propped against a fuel drum.

'PARKING de VOYAGE,' Ahmed read. Despite his tiredness, his regret at leaving his mother behind, and the ugliness of the place they'd reached, he had an involuntary thrill of anticipation. The real voyage to the land of plenty was about to begin.

From listening to the adults, he expected the crossings town to be a place of significance with Tarmac roads and street lighting. But it turned out to be no more than two rows of squat buildings facing each other across the sand. There were some low scrubby bushes and rubbish drifting in the wind. It was, however, busy with the bustle of comings and goings. Travellers arrived out of the dust-haze from the south and the east. Travellers who had organized the next stage of their trek were departing towards the north.

There were no traders from whom to buy supplies or provisions. There was only one place to eat, a canteen run by the same men who provided the travel permits. The price for bad food and fake documents was steep. The canteen was called Executives Departure Lounge Restaurant. Ahmed's uncle explained that this was humour. To further the joke, someone had added four stars and '*cuisine gastronomique*' to the canteen signboard.

At this desert outpost Ahmed heard many languages, for there were representatives from all over Africa, perhaps even, he guessed, from every nation of the world. From Senegal, Nigeria, Cameroon, Mali, Cote d'Ivoire and Liberia. From Burkina Faso, Guinea and Guinea Bissau, Arabs from Morocco, Tuaregs from Tunisia. The would-be travellers were all men. All had the same objective, to traverse the final stretch of land, and to reach the coast, then to sail to one of the European ports of plenty.

Ahmed saw one woman only, who stirred the great

cauldrons of floury stew in the canteen. This town was no place for women, let alone children. Ahmed tried to stand tall so that he might seem more like a man but he needn't have bothered. Nobody was interested in anything but their own acute problems of finance, hunger, or travel.

Ahmed was glad that he had his father and his uncle to protect him. His father told him, 'Our first task is to acquire appropriate papers and a carrier willing to convey us.' But it soon transpired that the man who prepared passports had run out of watermarked paper. The price of an exit visa stamp went up. So did the price of an identity photo. They stayed in the hostel above the canteen for more days than they had counted on. Beds, like meals at the canteen were not cheap. They shared a fly-blown room with eleven others. Among them were a Rwandan and a Zimbabwean, little older than Ahmed but they seemed unwilling or unable to speak with anybody else and each boy kept to himself. How had they managed to come so far on their own? What were they running from? Could their village have been as troubled as his own? Had they too left behind mothers and brothers?

At last, Ahmed's uncle located a transfer driver who'd offered, for only a small supplement, to take a route which would avoid passing the official checkpoint. No sooner had the deal been struck, than Ahmed's uncle heard that the driver had the reputation for transporting his customers directly to the checkpoints in order to collect a reward.

It was a risk they would have to take for the place buzzed with as many rumours as it did flies. Men, Ahmed heard, had died of thirst trying to reach the coast on foot. Men had died, right here, of starvation. Men who had been financed by their home village as an investment for the future, had been robbed of all but their shorts and were forced to work for slave-wages at the brick factory. Men caught with false papers had been robbed by the same officials who arrested them. The body of a missing Cameroonian had been found in a gully just over the horizon. The Algerians were the least corrupt transporters to deal with. No, not the Algerians, the Tunisians. No, not them, the Moroccans. The police were the most corrupt of all.

Ahmed was glad his father understood about the bribes, and knew how to manoeuvre through the maze of information and misinformation. But perhaps the strain was too much for him. Just as everything seemed ready for a safe departure, he fell sick. The site of the small wound in his thigh became hot. He could not put his weight on the leg. He needed the support of his brother on one side and his son on the other to walk a single step.

Anne-Marie's
Surprise

The weather continued damp with fog, obliging him to spend two days at home on his own with his schoolbooks, his flags and his classic motion-picture posters. Or nearly on his own. He had the impression that Douglas continued to lurk in the flat, not benignly to watch over him but to eavesdrop on his thoughts, to control him to his Scottish way of doing things.

When she came in, she was acting strangely, like a child with a secret. She kept glancing at him as he lay on the settee under his rug. As it was Wednesday, they were to have beans on toast for tea. He got up and opened the tin and heated the beans in a pan. She made the toast. She couldn't even do that very well. The toast was charred round the edges.

'Somesing's 'appened,' she said.

'That's all right,' he reassured her. 'We can cut the edges off.'

'Not the toasts. Somesing else.'

'Good or bad?' He had a sinking feeling that she might be about to reveal that she was going out on a date with a librarian.

'Somesing very good. Better san winning the lotto.'

He said, 'You can't win the lottery until you've bought a ticket first.' He smeared beans and red sauce to the edge of the toast to hide the burned bits. If you didn't see the black, you could pretend it wasn't there.

'I 'ave been offered a *bourse*.'

'A what?'

'A scholarship. Some money to study. My supervisor hadvised me to happly. I happlied. I am haccepted. To finish the dissertation.' A dissertation was like a class project only much longer. The worry about it had been hanging around, as invisible as Douglas now was, ever since Hamish could remember.

Anne-Marie waved a letter in the air. 'It is a residential scholarship. At the research centre.' She read aloud from the page, ' "Two consecutive semesters, with extension of third semester if the scholar's studies proceed satisfactorily and meet with the academic board's required levels of achievement." ' She tucked the letter back in its crisp envelope.

Hamish said, 'What about me?' Was he to be bundled off to the old woman in the damp dark north?

'You come too.' She tenderly placed her hand over his. 'Of course.'

'Do you think Douglas would have minded?'

' 'Ee is not 'ere.'

'He wouldn't have let you go though, would he?'

'We cannot live hin the past,' said Anne-Marie, like Ms Florence at school kept saying. 'We 'ave to move on.' She quoted from her letter again. 'And with a small allowance. About three hundred pounds each month. So not so much. But not so little sat we can't be 'appy.'

Hamish didn't know how any of this might affect his own life. It was unsettling.

'It means we are going far away. Where I will do all my reading all day and you will become bonny and braw like the grandmother Heather wishes.'

Hamish wondered, would they go far enough to elude Douglas's eerie presence, or would he follow them forever?

Ahmed's Father

He was head of the family. He was firm in his authority. 'The two of you will continue the voyage we have begun. I will remain here. The paperwork is resolved. All necessary payments have been made. There will be no trouble.'

Ahmed's uncle refused to accept the brother's orders and change of plan. Ahmed too spoke out against his father. 'If you stay, there's nobody to look after you!' He meant, but did not need to say aloud, If we leave you here, you will die here.

Ahmed's uncle said, 'That is so. The people here are only interested in arranging their own crossing. They have family worries of their own. They can't worry about you.'

The older man said, 'What I say is what we will do. We will not risk the success of the trip. When you arrive and have work, you will send for me. I will not be staying here. I will go with one of the returning truck-drivers.'

He was talking nonsense. They all knew that in this unregulated no-man's-land, no driver, even with an empty truck, would transport a sick passenger without a plump fee. Ahmed's uncle said, 'It is rumoured that when they suspect a passenger has more money hidden in his clothing, they will rob him before pushing him out in the middle of the night. You *have* to come with us. Only you know what we must do when we reach the other side.'

Anne Marie
and Hamish

She said, 'And anusser sing. You will need your passport.' She sounded it in the French way, without a T at the end.

'Passport!' He had assumed that by 'going far away', she'd meant Scotland and he knew perfectly well that he didn't need a passport to cross the invisible line separating Northumberland from the Scottish Borders.

Acquiring the death certificate for Douglas had involved Anne-Marie in so many official visits that Hamish supposed this would be similar. But it turned out to be no big deal. She fetched an application form from the post office. She filled it in. She and Hamish drove to the big supermarket. The automatic photo-booth was by the entrance, near where the shopping trolleys were lined up. She combed his hair flat. She told him to sit on the rotating stool inside the booth. This faced a rectangular glass which turned out to be more than a mirror for checking your appearance. This was the camera's eye. It flashed four times. Four times Hamish blinked and five minutes later four head-and-shoulder pictures of a startled Hamish emerged from the slot.

Anne-Marie took two of the photos to the doctor's surgery. She left them with the receptionist who got the doctor to sign the back to guarantee that this was indeed a true likeness of the individual and that he had known him for at least two years. Anne-Marie then wrote a cheque, put everything in an envelope and sent it off.

A short while later, the passport arrived in a brown envelope. Maroon cover with gold block printing on the cover. EUROPEAN COMMUNITY UNITED KINGDOM OF GREAT BRITAIN AND NORTHERN IRELAND was printed across the top half. In the centre of the front page was the image of a crowned lion rearing up on its hind legs, and a unicorn wearing its crown around its neck. Together, they were supporting a shield with a harp and seven more lions, wrapped round with a buckled belt. This was topped by the largest crown of all. All in gold, as though confirming the fact that the Queen was the richest person in the country.

Inside, in curly script, Hamish read, 'Her Britannic

Majesty's Secretary of State Requests and requires in the Name of Her Majesty all those whom it may concern to allow the bearer to pass freely without let or hindrance and to afford the bearer such assistance and protection as may be necessary.'

He turned to the back to check the photo. It had been stamped with a rose crown, and was embalmed under plastic film. The image of a startled rabbit caught in car head-lights was hardly him. He saw his name, birthdate and place of birth. Anne-Marie had filled it in.

'You've put London,' he said.

She nodded.

'But I was born in Scotland.'

'I never told you sat, 'Amish. Douglas would have *liked* you to 'ave been born in Scotland. Sat is all. But because, because.' She hesitated. 'Because of circumstances at sat time, you har born in North London.'

'Oh.' He was relieved. To have been born in a separate country distanced him from Douglas more thoroughly than death had so far done. He returned to his study of the two pages of notes in ant-sized print, about validity, immigration and visa requirements, dual nationality. He learned that although this passport had his name in it, and his own individual nine-digit number, it did not belong to him. It remained the property of Her Majesty's Government in the United Kingdom. So what would happen if her government suddenly wanted all their passports back? Like, on a sudden whim, people demand the return of all the CDs or best comics they've lent out? Where would the government put their reclaimed passports? Did they have a special passport library? How big would it have to be? In London alone there were over seven million people and if only one-seventh of those people were each in possession of one of her majesty's government's passports and returned it when asked, it would require a massive amount of space to shelve them.

Anne-Marie said, 'You must sign it. It's not valid if it's not signed. No, not in pencil. In pen, so it can't be changed.'

'Suppose somebody couldn't write their own name? Say they were too young or just didn't know how?'

Anne-Marie smiled. 'Sen her majesty's government would haccept a signature on their behalf, by their muzzer.'

Hamish memorized his passport number. He re-inspected his signature, wishing his handwriting were less childishly neat. Too late now. There wasn't room to cross it out and try again with a more adult-looking scrawl. Moreover, one of the regulation notes stated that this governmental property was not to be tampered with.

Till now, he had been unaware of the absence of, or need for, a passport, since he knew perfectly who he thought he was. And even now he'd got it, it didn't seem much of thing, just a pocket-sized booklet with a tacky plastic covering and some machine-stitching down the middle to hold the pages together, which could easily be unpicked.

Yet now that this had been issued, and he held it in his hand, it gave him an unexpected sense of inner strength, a confirmation of his significance as an individual in the world. Well all right, not in the whole world, but in Great Britain. He was one of the fifty-nine and a half million citizens of Britain who had the right to roam the world. Okay, so not the *whole* world since there might be parts in North Korea, Zimbabwe, the Middle East, or China where he wouldn't be welcome. Elsewhere, he would have the reassurance that, should he fall into difficulties, he had the power and the protection of the authorities or consuls or representatives of the United Kingdom right behind him and that felt good.

What should have felt good, but felt odd, was the next piece of information to come his way which was that he wasn't a Scot and never had been.

Anne-Marie said, 'I am going to make a pot hoff coffee and Douglas was your stepfather.' It was fast-track, all in the same sentence.

'What?' he said, in the oafish way that Douglas used so often to correct. He'd just received a confirmation of one aspect of his identity. Two seconds later, another aspect of what he thought of as himself was removed. Peculiar. Confusing. He had been unnecessarily contaminated with Douglas's Scottishness. But from now on, he could forget all about him and just be himself. 'So thank goodness.'

'Sank goodness?'

'Thank goodness I've got this passport now. Now I can travel anywhere in the world I want, can't I?'

'Not wisout my permission, till you are sixteen,' said Anne-Marie.

Ahmed and the Very Young Doctor from Bruxelles

Ahmed overheard in the canteen how there was a travellers' medical centre. It seemed unlikely. Even in his village there had been no regular medical centre. Doubtingly, he went in search. He found the sign of the Red Crescent on the white background on a painted notice attached to the grey-brick mud wall. This indicated the clinic. Already, a queue of men of all ages and conditions, who Ahmed took to be the sick people, was snaking along outside the room. Through the open door Ahmed saw a small windowless room, bare but for a metal cupboard, bent metal chair and metal table.

Ahmed fetched his father and his uncle. All three joined the tail of the queue and within a few moments more people joined behind them. The wait seemed long. It was so hot and dusty. Each time another arriving or a departing truck went past, it threw up clouds of dusty sand. When it was their turn to go into the medical room, Ahmed's uncle suddenly decided he did not trust the doctor, even though he was wearing a white clinician's coat and new leather sandals. But his appearance was young and, unlike most of the residents of this strange town, both the temporary and the long-term, he was not grey with dust.

Ahmed's uncle muttered, 'So there is water for him to wash himself, even though there is scarcely enough for us to drink.' It was true. The crossings town seemed to Ahmed like the very driest place in the world. Ahmed's uncle did not bother with making a formal greeting but at once demanded of the man in the white coat, 'How can we trust that you are a genuine hakim?'

Ahmed felt embarrassed. But the man in the white coat didn't appear offended. He said, 'I am not a hakim. I am a western-style physician.' He explained that he was a Tuareg from Tunisia and that he had been trained in Belgium.

Ahmed's uncle said, 'Very well. So how much will this cost?'

'There is no consultation fee.'

Ahmed's uncle said, 'Then how can you stay here if you don't belong here and if nobody is paying you for the treatment you offer?'

'I am supported to be here by an international humanitarian agency. They pay me monthly. So far, they have not failed.'

Ahmed's uncle was disconcerted that any man would be here if he did not have to be. He said, 'Very well. You may now look at my brother's leg.'

With great thoroughness, the Tuareg examined Ahmed's father, not just the wounded leg, but all over. He said, 'You are seriously malnourished. And you have anaemia. You must eat two meals a day. As for the wound, I can clean and dress it. Then you must go quickly to a properly equipped hospital for help.'

Ahmed's father said, 'There are strong drugs that will cure anything. We will pay you.'

The doctor said, 'I can give you some antibiotics to help slow the infection. But they cannot halt it. This is no longer a superficial wound. It has become contaminated.'

Ahmed's uncle said, 'But you have cleaned it. Tell me how, and I will clean it every day.'

The doctor said, 'It is too late for that. My diagnosis is gas gangrene. I have nothing here to treat this. You need a surgeon. I am not a surgeon. Look around. What do you see? Almost nothing. Not even refrigeration for the drugs.'

Ahmed's father said, 'There must be someone here who will help us?'

'The people who run this town are not welfare workers. Surely you can see they are running a business. A multi-million-dollar global business. Once the trade was slavery. Now it's no better. Today's enterprise is smuggling. You are just dots in their commercial empire.'

When he had finished dressing the wound, he spoke directly to Ahmed's uncle. 'Friend, my sincere advice to you is to get your brother to a hospital and send the boy back to where you are from. However bad it was there, it is nothing to what you face ahead. You may think the conditions here are poor, but, believe me, I have heard it is worse at other transit towns.'

The uncle listened without giving any indication that he agreed or disagreed. The doctor went on, 'You travellers are all so very stubborn. Nobody here listens to reason, no matter how I describe the dangers. All around us, there is civil war. And ahead you think there's peace, but the European countries are growing more hostile. These days, they can arrest a man for doing nothing but arriving!'

Ahmed wasn't sure who to believe. But he felt, from his own limited experience, that going back to where there was no paid work, where the school had been ransacked, where people were scared to tend the crops, where the militia with their guns went roaring around like madmen, did not seem like a wise option. Having started this journey, he wanted to continue with it, to reach the lands of plenty where there was enough water and food, and where education was valued and enforced in the way that Monsieur Bruno had once explained. There were countries whose laws obliged children to attend school until they were sixteen years old, where parents were punished if they kept their children out of the class to help at home or in the fields. If Ahmed reached one of those countries, then his desire to train as a teacher was not a naive dream but could become reality.

The doctor tried one more time to convince the adults of the difficulties ahead. 'And if my diagnosis is wrong and you make it to the coast, what happens if you are stranded at sea? The Mediterranean is wide and deep.'

Ahmed's uncle said, with such authority and confidence that Ahmed supposed he must know what he was talking about, 'Here, on dry land, to help one's fellow man – as you are doing – is an act of admirable altruism even if it is not necessarily normal or legally required. At sea, the situation has always been different. Before setting out, my brother studied this.

Assistance on the oceans is never an act of philanthropy. It has been written into maritime law since Roman times. It is the obligation of all seafarers to assist those who cross their path, whether those in need of help are marooned in a stricken craft or already in the water. The Mediterranean is a network of shipping lines. From Tripoli to Tunis. Ajaccio to Algiers. Valletta to Malaga. Barcelona to Naples. Palermo to Marseille.'

The mention of so many exotic ports increased Ahmed's excitement. Perhaps they would actually get to see the Blue Mosque, the Alhambra Palace, the Egyptian pyramids, the Arc de Triomphe.

'So even if, by some terrible mischance,' Ahmed's uncle concluded, 'the craft that we sail on turns out to be unseaworthy, we are certain to be rescued.'

The doctor sighed and shook his head. 'Such obstinate men,' he said.

The bandaging of the leg was done. Ahmed's father stood and smiled as proof of his fitness to travel. It seemed to Ahmed that his uncle was right and the doctor was certainly young enough to have made a wrong diagnosis. They gave the doctor their greeting of farewell. The doctor gave his. The three travellers left the clinic.

The next patient was waiting to come in. He had a

persistent cough. The doctor suspected pneumonia. There was nothing he could do. He knew this patient was soon to die, whereas the previous fellow had a chance.

Hamish, Bon Voyage

Further confirmation of his freakiness came on Hamish's last day at school. His class tutor gave him a quick nod, and said, 'Good luck, lad, in your new life,' but nobody else, staff or boys, bothered to say goodbye. He wondered, was he invisible as well as different?

No, not invisible unless Watkins had heat-seeking eyes, for outside the cloakrooms, he sidled up to him and pushed a small, warm packet into Hamish's hand.

'Goodbye present. For your journey. Mum said it would be okay. Don't suppose they'll have this type of chocolate where you're going.'

'As a matter of fact,' Hamish replied grandly, 'they have very good chocolate over there, specially Swiss and Austrian.' He saw Watkins's crestfallen face and suddenly wondered why, every time poor Dim Tim offered him something, or tried to be extra helpful, he'd made some unnecessarily negative remark. Why had he been so consistently harsh? Hamish couldn't understand it. He knew it was wrong to bully weak people. Yet the kinder Dim Tim had tried to be, the more something inside Hamish became cold and spiky. He thought, At least now was a chance, if not exactly to apologize for months of bad humour, at least to accept the gift and say something half decent.

'Hey, milk chocolate buttons! Fantastic! My favourite. Ta very much.'

Watkins beamed as though he was the one who'd been given the present.

'So this is it. Be seeing you then,' Hamish said.

Watkins took a step closer and touched his arm. He went pink in the face. He said, 'I'm really going to miss you, Hamish. I'm glad you're going to wherever it is, for your sake. But I wish I knew you were definitely coming back.'

'Yep,' said Hamish. 'I know what you mean. It's the uncertainty.' A week ago, he might have thought, Better to have no friends at all than an encumbrance like Watkins. Now, with the unknown future only a day away, he wasn't so sure. 'Well, it's goodbye then. Maybe I'll send you a postcard.'

He strode through the school gates, passing a group of boys just outside. They were from his class. They studiously ignored him. He wondered, was it about him kicking that girl from the other school? Or was it his consistently high marks which none of them could match? Were they simply glad to see the back of him so that one of them might get their chance to be top?

He walked to the bus stop for the final time with a sinking feeling in his stomach. Dreary though this current place was, incomprehensible though its inhabitants were, at least there was familiarity. The new life might be better, but on the other hand, it might well be far worse.

On the Road

He couldn't help staring in awe at the foreignness of France. The electric pylons and telegraph poles were of a different design. The farm buildings, too, had a different slant to their roofs. She was nervous about the driving. They were travelling on what felt like the wrong side of the road so that, from the passenger seat, the oncoming traffic seemed to be coming directly at him. He was supposed to be navigating.

She said, 'This can't be right. There is supposed to be an autoroute, right after we leave the tunnel terminus. How can we have missed it?'

He scrabbled with the map, trying to work out where they were. They were on a country road but he couldn't find it on the map. 'Sorry.'

Anne-Marie pulled to an abrupt halt. He thought she wanted a turn with the map. But she wound down her window and stared out at a green treeless plain. 'There!' she said, pointing. 'Right there!'

'What?' said Hamish. 'What are we meant to be looking at it?'

'The camp. It's over there.'

'What camp?'

In the distance he could see a grey military hangar of the type that might once have housed fighter planes.

He said, 'Doesn't look like a camp.' At the class camping week, they'd gone to a place with bright chalets and coloured flags between the trees. Because of the asthma, he'd had to attend as a day-boy so missed out on the disco and late-night pranks.

She said, 'It must be where they're putting them now.'

'Putting who?'

'They have to put them somewhere. Of course they do.'

Who was she talking about? He said, 'Do you mean homeless people?'

She said, 'They call them by so many names. The refugees. The sans-papiers. The stateless. Whatever they call them, they cannot leave them without shelter. That would not be correct. They are not animals. I do not agree with their actions.' Now she was talking about the people in authority, whoever they were. Then she was back onto the homeless people. 'They are troublesome to everybody in every country. But I am sorry for them, poor miserable souls. There was a camp like that near a village called Sangatte. The British closed it down. And now they have had to open another one. So much muddle and waste.'

She drove forward again till they were on a lane that ran alongside the hangar. There was a wire fence round it, strung with windblown rubbish. The plastic bags and the Red Cross signboard were the only bright colours. As they passed near the entrance to the hangar, Hamish saw lines of smaller tents inside the large one. Four children stood at the entrance, hardly moving, just staring impassively at Anne-Marie and Hamish's car.

'Such desolation,' said Anne-Marie. 'Too much of desolation. This is a too sad destination for them, whoever they are. They must be expecting a welcome so much better.' Hamish wasn't sure if she was crying or angry as she accelerated down the lane away from the hangar. Two women with babies slung in shawls round their shoulders had to leap like chickens into the grass verge.

Hamish said, 'Are those Turks then?'

Anne-Marie said sharply, 'The Turks? How should I know? But whoever they are, the sight of them is depressing. We should not have come this way. Take more care with the map-reading from now on or I will have to see to it myself.'

When they were finally bowling along the autoroute, she became less apprehensive. And map-reading was no longer necessary. But she would never drive after dark.

'Never again in my life.'

They stopped in a market town. Hamish had not stayed in a hotel before. Douglas had distrusted them. 'Why pay good money to lie in a stranger's bed?' he had said. In one sense he had been right. The beds were dusty. Hamish had a wheezy night but was cheered by hot drinking chocolate and warm butter croissants for breakfast. While Anne-Marie was paying the bill, he watched the television in the reception lounge.

On screen, uniformed guards were advancing on a crowd of people. Another view showed figures on horseback charging into a crowd. A woman stumbled on the kerb and fell. One of the men began hitting her on her back with a baton. Then there were several small explosions and clouds of smoke and the people were scattering in all directions.

Hamish changed channels but they were showing the same images. Security people were chasing other people down narrow streets. People were falling over each other when there wasn't room to escape. And billows of white smoke. It was mesmerizing. The commentary was in French, spoken fast. Hamish could only follow some of it. This wasn't a drama. It was live news. He thought he was seeing the outbreak of a war which nobody had told him about.

The hotel manager glanced across at the television screen.

'Ah, Paris,' he said, in a matter-of-fact way. 'The riots. Those Parisians, always having demonstrations. They cannot resist. Actors' pay. Beef. Leopard-skin fashion. Anything that takes their fancy. Today, migrants. Students demonstrate over migrants. What next! These things are ridiculous. But out here in the provinces we enjoy life. Let and let live. Not to worry, young man. Paris is far off.'

Anne-Marie turned to look at the screen. 'But we have to go through Paris! And they're using tear-gas! That is bad. My son has a breathing problem.'

The manager nodded. 'Madame, you are right. That is not a situation for visitors to be in. Those who have no business in the capital would be well advised to avoid it.'

'But I *do* have business there. I have ordered important research material from the Bibliothèque Nationale. I have a rendezvous with the curator to collect it.'

'Madame,' said the hotelier, smiling as if advising on a good resort rather than on avoidance of streets riots,

'You are travelling south and I strongly recommend that you give notice of your delay to those awaiting you at your rendez-vous and you take the other autoroute. It is as good. Even better. When my wife and I go south in August, we always take the A17.'

The hotelier offered her the use of his telephone. Hamish listened as she requested her research materials be sent south by post. She was speaking, as she had to the hotel manager, in French and fluently. She sounded normal. He didn't need to be embarrassed about people hearing her peculiar accent. Here she had no accent. She was no longer an outsider.

They avoided Paris and the riots. They drove for four hours. Then they came off the autoroute and she stopped at a restaurant. On the dashboard clock, it showed one minute past twelve.

'Midi! Déjeuner!' she announced.

Hamish understood, though felt too shy to respond in French.

'Dinner time?' he said in English. 'But it's only just twelve o'clock.'

She persisted in the language of her childhood. 'Ici, c'est la France. À midi, we eat.'

He had not expected she'd be able to transpose to her original identity so rapidly. Yet language and appropriate behaviour seemed to be coming naturally to her without stress. Eating in restaurants, cafés, snack-bars, fast-food outlets, had never been supported by Douglas. 'I do not earn a daily wage to waste on paying others to dither around serving uneatable food which one can perfectly well have at home at half the price.' So, due to Anne-Marie's incompetence as a cook, Hamish's most frequently consumed meal was toast with eggs, either fried, poached, boiled or scrambled, and which he himself prepared.

Even if it was only three minutes past twelve, or past eleven, English time, Hamish was hungry. It was exciting to be led across a restaurant to a table and seated, with the prospect of a three-course déjeuner ahead. He appreciated the way it seemed so normal. He tried to look as though he was accustomed to it. At the other tables, sat other normal people, couples, men in suits, two gendarmes, three men with muddy boots, all normally eating or waiting to eat. Why hadn't he come to France before? If this was what one could do everybody should be doing it.

'Thanks, Mum,' he said across the gingham tablecloth. 'It's cool.'

She smiled. 'This is just an ordinary restaurant. Nothing special.'

A television perched on the buffet at one end of the salon. More news. The Paris demos hadn't escalated. All over. Streets back to normal, choked with traffic. The lead item was the couture shows. A top couturier was presenting a knitted chador for men. The prototype was shown being modelled on the catwalk.

'Looks like a crusader's coif,' Hamish giggled.

Anne-Marie smiled. 'Chain-mail,' she said.

The waiter brought their first course. Hamish felt happy.

'Merci, Maman,' he said slowly. 'Je suis très content.'

The pâté de Bruxelles sat neat, pink and appetizing on the white china plate, decorated with a gherkin, sliced delicately into a palm-tree shape.

The dark green gherkin beside the pork pâté made Hamish nauseous. He pushed it to one side to hide it under the fork. The smell it gave off made him know he would throw up long before the arrival of the bœuf en daube.

Anne-Marie
and Her Lover

No map-reading required. Clear autoroutes swooped southwards. They sped through countryside which was rich, varied and fertile. Ms Florence's facts rattled through his brain. Thirty-three per cent arable. Thirty-two million tonnes of wheat per year. Five million, three hundred thousand tonnes of wine.

Stuck together in the car, travelling at a hundred and ten kilometres an hour between their sad shared past and their unknown futures, the relationship was becoming closer than Hamish might have liked. She was in confidential mood.

'I suppose,' she said, breaking into considerations about why a liquid like wine came to be measured in tonnes rather than litres or bottles, 'you will often have wondered why Douglas was your stepfather.'

Was this a statement or a question? He knew his response would be a vehement, No. When you told me he wasn't my biological father, he would have said, I was relieved. It meant I could forget about him, not have to think about him. So right now I am thinking about France as the world's leading agricultural exporter of beef and sheep.

Too abrupt. He hesitated. 'Maybe.' Why deliberately hurt her feelings? Try to be kind to her. He'd given brutal replies to too many people. He could dilute past cruelties with a bit of gentleness. Besides, was she about to reveal some other secret that he had always suspected? He was not her true son? He had been conceived, on a Petri dish in a laboratory of unknown donors? He was found under a gooseberry bush? Picked out of a rush basket on the Nile? He did not want to know the answer.

What was important was that twenty-five per cent of grassland-grazing supported twenty million French cattle, ten million sheep, fourteen and a half million pigs, and one point twenty million goats.

It was too late to deflect her from the tale she had begun. 'So I went to London as an au pair, a cheap child-nurse. I was not yet eighteen. My employers were kind when they had time. But they were busy lawyers. They had no time for their child. No time for me. I was lonely. I met a young man, Gustave, in a coffee-house. He was studying at a language school.'

'And he is my father?'

'No. His friend.'

'What was his name?'

The traffic on the autoroute was thickening. Three near-empty lanes of traffic were reducing to one.

'Watch out! Slow down!' he shouted. 'Get over into the other lane.'

Trucks thundered by at speed on either side, then braked ahead. Emergency tail-lights were flashing. Anne-Marie manoeuvred down the narrow gorge of steel. The hazard was a double-decker transporter carrying a load of sheep, which had overturned. Ripped tyres, torn metal and hysterical bleating came from the slatted vents. Several dozen of the country's sheep population had been deleted from the head-count in a single moment of careless driving.

Well past the hold-up Anne-Marie's hands became less tightly clamped to the steering-wheel. To Hamish's regret, she took up her story.

'We went to the same evening class centre. Marylebone. Douglas took pity on me. Such a strange name!'

Douglas or Marylebone?

'I was doing the computers. He was studying genealogy. He had to discover which clang he belonged to.'

'Clang?'

'Yes. The tribe. With their own chief.'

'Ah. Clan.' Clearly some significant details, more important than which clan Douglas claimed as his own, had got lost in the snarl-up of injured and dying sheep. He didn't ask for clarification. He knew who Douglas was. That was enough information for the time being. He hadn't invited this bewildering unburdening.

'I didn't belong to any place. I wanted so much to belong.'

Why reveal this stuff now?

'And he offered to marry me. I hardly knew him. I was so young. I was convent-educated. Mother Superior would have never been able to even look at me without feeling contaminated by my sin. Christianity is a very unforgiving faith. No Hail Marys would expurgate my transgression. He was a good man. You must never forget it.' She was speaking fluently and fast. She'd slid into French almost without him noticing. 'But to be pitied, well, that is difficult to bear. You see, we were so alone in the world, just the two of us. Like now. I believed it would be good for you to have a father. Perhaps I should have had more patience and more courage.'

Hamish had never expected it would be necessary to

identify with the emotional crisis of a young pregnant woman who happened to be his biological mother. He said, 'Why didn't you just go home?'

'You know I had no home to go to. You know my parents were gone.'

Yes, if he concentrated he remembered but for how long was one supposed to hang on to the ghosts of long-ago people who were rarely mentioned? Anne-Marie's father had always sounded like a selfish slob. He'd abandoned Anne-Marie's mother, sailed across the Big Pond, tried his luck in a Pittsburgh factory and never been heard from again. Anne-Marie's mother went crazy and was put into an institution for the mentally deranged. It was a tough story. No wonder she wasn't keen on retelling it every night.

'My grandparents were country people. They took me to the house of orphans, The Shelter for Little Souls. There, the Sisters needed me for they no longer had sufficient unparented children to fill their shelter and to justify their own existence.'

If only he were older he could share the driving and she could go to sleep.

'We didn't belong. Like we are now. Just the two of us, alone. It was a bad time. It is better not to think of it.'

It wasn't *me* that first started on about your past, he thought, but kept to himself.

'This time, once again, it is just the two of us and we must enjoy the good times ahead.'

What good times ahead? He had a slurping sickness at the top of his stomach which increased when they reached the autoroute toll barrier. The pay booth was on Hamish's side. Anne-Marie explained to him what to do, in French. She went on speaking in French for the rest of the day. He was embarrassed, not by her, but by himself because he only dared reply in English.

'Don't worry, Hamish, you will find it becomes easier once you get going.' Curiously, in French, she could say his name without losing the H.

Why would a mother, his mother, give her baby a name that she couldn't pronounce?

She said, 'The name I chose was Henri. But Douglas he wanted Hamish. And it is a good name, is it not?'

Such an essential change had been made without him even knowing about it. Suppose he *had* been called Henri, might he have ended up a different kind of person?

SEA
CHANGE

Hamish, the Resolute

Happiness can come to those who don't merit it as easily as it can to those who do. (Hamish remembered Douglas dourly stating this fact when a younger colleague had been promoted over his head.)

Their happiness claimed them out of the blue. At first, unaccustomed to contentment, Hamish didn't recognize it for what it was. He had been dozing. He woke to see a bleak, rock-strewn plateau. A bird of prey circled in a lowering sky. The road was narrow.

'Not much further,' Anne-Marie faltered, unconvincingly. 'I think.' She spoke in French, otherwise she would have said, I sink, which would have been closer to the feelings of both of them.

This desolate terrain was not promising. Hamish suspected that they might end up in some hangar like that curious encampment near Calais. Here, no sign of human life, no buildings, not even shelters for high-pasture sheep or goats. So where did they graze their twelve million sheep and their seven point five million milking goats?

'Not like I was expecting,' he grumbled. But what *had* he been expecting? His geographical knowledge of France was all data and statistics, neatly lined up in columns.

Might not a normal boy have been uneasy about travelling for two days and a thousand kilometres to an unknown destination where he wouldn't know a soul? Hamish reminded himself that he had never been a normal boy. He was unlike all other boys. He was truly exceptional.

They reached a narrow pass between two daunting cliff-faces. Beyond, was a momentary glimpse of grey, then it was gone as the road tumbled into the shadow of the valley, zigzagging between pine-covered escarpments, a critical bend near the bottom as it angled round a boulder and on the big rock perched a church and on the church an ironwork bell-tower and on the tower sat two doves, white against a vast dark sea.

'Oh!' she cried. Then again, 'Oh, oh!'

'Oh, what?'

They entered a village and she had to slow to walking pace. The main street was scarcely wider than the car. She said uncertainly, 'I suppose we are allowed here?' As though he'd know the answer! 'We haven't passed any signs to say we can't, have we?'

He hated it when she was hesitant. It usually led to disintegration with weeping.

Two men in tattered shorts and rubber boots carried a basket of fish, still flapping, towards them. Anne-Marie leaned across Hamish to ask them the way. But they had already disappeared between two leaning houses.

Hamish felt uncomfortable. He was going to tell her to reverse out the way they'd come, but suddenly they were spat out, like a pip from an orange, on to the waterfront. They were a hair's breadth from the edge. No other cars. She must have been right. This wasn't the way to come.

Ahead, right in their eyes, was the sun, big and red like Mars. It was sliding into the sea from a drape of purple cloud. The harbour water rippled like gold foil. The houses round the harbour faced into the sunset like hellebores. They were pink, ochre, yellow and vermillion, each retaining their own tint, yet also glowing in red unity. It was like magic, but Hamish was not yet bewitched. He was overawed. His hand gripped the side of the seat. Not his right hand, just the left where she couldn't see it.

The quayside cafés were busy. So was the oyster stall,

decorated with lemons and black seaweed. People strolled, arm in arm. Children raced on scooters and nobody yelled at them about falling into the golden water. A red-sailed yacht slid silently towards its mooring.

Who had made this extraordinary scene? Was it for real?

She too was gazing at the shimmering water and the smouldering sky, then dropped her head on to the steering wheel and her shoulders began to heave. Signal for imminent emotional collapse.

'Oh Maman. Not.all that again.' But she was smiling, even laughing at the same time.

'Nous sommes arrivés!' She wiped her eyes. She gave him a hug. 'I do not believe it. I cannot believe that we are here!' She blew her nose before asking directions from a waiter at one of the cafés.

Home Sweet Mimosa

The Institut was easy to spot, a local landmark on the coast, set in luxuriant tropical gardens. The decorative gates opened automatically.

'Stupefying!' she said.

A servant came down the villa steps to greet them.

'Bonjour madame. Bonjour, Hamish,' he said.

'They know my name!' Hamish whispered in English.

'Bienvenue. You are both most welcome here. I am Pierre, personal assistant to Monsieur le Directeur. Follow me, s'il vous plaît.' He gathered up two of their cases and Anne-Marie's carton of books and led the way into the villa. They crossed a marble hall, then proceeded up a curved stairway.

'Stupefying!' said Anne-Marie. 'This is all so truly stupefying.'

When would she find a new adjective to express her pleasure?

'Here is your apartment, madame. Les Mimosas,' the man said. 'You will find your welcome pack in your kitchen. It contains all you might require for immediate use. Here too is your information pack. If you require assistance, please come to the office in the main building where I, or another member of administrative staff, will do our best to help you. Now you will wish to rest from your journey. The Scholars' Orientation Meeting will take place in the Grande Salle at eight-thirty.' He handed Anne-Marie a set of keys. 'Bonsoir.' He shook her and Hamish by the hand and left, closing the apartment door quietly behind him.

'Can you believe it? It's called Les Mimosas!' Anne-Marie breathed as though the name were a spell.

'Funny name for a flat. Sounds like those Indian pastry things.'

'Samosas. Mimosa is a flower. Yellow blossom and elusive perfume that speaks to the world of springtime. Stupefying!'

She sank to the tiled floor and lay with closed eyes. She was obviously still overcome by the pretty sunset. Or had she fainted from the heat?

It was warm. And she'd been driving all day, straight into the sun. Perhaps she was dehydrated and that's why she was talking nonsense. He knew about dehydration.

One time in A & E, a marathon runner was rushed in and put in the next cubicle. They resuscitated her with fluids. He'd heard it through the screens and wanted to take a peek but he'd been all tubed up himself. She'd recovered ahead of him. He heard her say she wanted to rejoin the race. They wouldn't let her. They made her go home in a taxi.

If they were at home, he'd have brewed up a pot of tea. But they were not home. They were beside the Mediterranean in the south of France in a flat named after some special blossom which was not a sunflower.

He found the welcome pack, a wicker basket filled with ready-to-eat provisions. How had the directorship known that Anne-Marie scarcely knew how to boil an egg? Were all Scholars like that?

They'd kept the dehydrated marathon runner conscious by going on talking to her, on and on about anything and nothing. He unpacked the basket and talked. 'Two bottles of wine. One white, one red. Bottle opener. Jar of something dark. Morello conserve. Jar of something black. Thick, like tar. Some kind of paste.' He unscrewed the top. 'Smells of olives.'

'Tapenade,' she murmured from the floor. 'Local speciality.'

'Thank you. Ground coffee. Breadstick.'

'Baguette.'

123

'Very well. Baguette. Croissants. Cheese, creamy. Smells like dog poo. Bag of fruit. Peaches.'

Not a whisper of a tea bag. He had never tried to open a wine bottle and had an intuition that it wasn't appropriate for rehydration.

In her dreamy trance, she raised a hand to accept a glass of tap water. 'Stupefying,' she said.

So she was okay. He said in English, 'Astonishing, surprising, inexplicable, wonderful, contrary to expected information, incredible, mind-boggling, astounding, remarkable, miraculous and staggering are all useful alternatives.' He made her drink three tumblers of water. 'You'll live,' he said, which was what Douglas always said when Hamish had come through another crisis. 'I'm going down to fetch the rest of the stuff.'

In the parking lot under the palms, a gangly young man approached. 'Bonsoir, monsieur,' said Hamish and instinctively held out his right hand.

'Hey,' the man drawled in reply.

Hamish said nothing.

'Hey, I'm Ned. You a noo Scholar too?'

'Um, yes. Er, that is, no. I'm with someone who is doing her doctorate on caterpillars and medieval religion.'

A young woman sauntered under the palm trees

towards them. 'Hey, hey,' she trilled to Ned, ignoring Hamish. 'Spotted you at the airport.'

'Hey,' said Ned.

Hamish thought, This is going to be easy as sawdust. English spoken. Vocabulary basic.

'Say, say,' said the young woman to the man. 'Didn't reckon on little kids being around, did you? That's real neat.'

Ned nodded towards Hamish. 'Yup. He'll stop us getting too seriously embedded in our studies, won't you, son?'

Hamish said, 'My mother is serious with her studies.'

The young woman winked at the young man.

'Then, hey, hey, if Mom's about we better watch our step, uhuh?' he said and winked back at her.

Were they laughing with him or at him? Either way, it didn't feel comfortable. He lugged the rest of the luggage up the stairs. In the apartment, he unpacked his flag collection, selected four favourites, and hung them across the room. Mali (green, yellow and red). Togo (green and yellow stripes with white star). Democratic Republic of Congo (diagonal green and yellow with stripes of green with a red crescent and star). Burkina Faso (red and green with star). He had little idea where these countries were but he knew their bold flag colours so intimately he could have reproduced them blindfold.

The ceiling was high. The flags swayed in the warm air current but didn't make him feel secure. How could he make this bizarre place feel like a home sweet home?

He unpacked his prime film poster, The Wages of Fear. It showed a grim man with dark eyes but strong arms. Perhaps his familiar face might help.

Point du Départ

They reached the coast in the north of the great continent, expecting to leave immediately. Instead, they spent three interminable days waiting. As the doctor had predicted, conditions were far worse at the port than during their stay at the desert crossings town. They slept in a waterfront warehouse. It had formerly been used for the storage of phosphates and phosphoric acid, prior to shipment. Now the chief freight was live men. Those who were making their fortunes from this trade were in no hurry to pass the men on. In the warehouse, there were no beds, no bed-rolls, no blankets. Cardboard packing cases and plastic sacks were made available to buy or hire by the night. They helped protect one's body from the hard concrete.

Inside the warehouse was an atmosphere of permanent tension. Transactions were conducted at night. Departure would also be at night. By day travellers lay on their sacks or their strip of cardboard and waited for the signal that their payments had been approved and their departure time had come.

The shed was overcrowded. No friendship was squandered between fellow men. Each was watching out for his own back. Travellers stole from fellow travellers when they slept, even as they bent to pick up their belongings.

When the uncle went out to the Msalla for prayers, the boy went with him. The old man was too weak.

'Praise be to God, Lord of the worlds, the compassionate, the merciful, king of the day of judgement, you do we worship and your aid do we seek.' The boy said the words. None of his family had ever made the pilgrimage to Mecca. Perhaps, if he and the uncle earned enough in the land of plenty, they would one day make the hajj.

The people-smugglers had already been paid when suddenly there were demands for further payments before transportation. 'Unforeseen circumstances' and 'additional expenses' had to be covered. The boy realized that the two men who constituted his family no longer knew which were the smugglers to be trusted, which were emigration authorities, which were spies pretending to be one thing and waiting to denounce you. Those false travel documents which had cost no little effort and very much money were no guarantee of the type of craft which would convey them on the final leg of their journey. It might be a schooner, a clipper, a trawler, one of the small ferries that serviced the oil rigs, a coracle, a leaking tub or a rubber dingy as full of holes as a cabbage-strainer. The boy heard all of these vessels under discussion in the warehouse. He wouldn't be able to identify one from the other and suspected that his uncle wouldn't either. And anyway, in the darkness of night, what difference would it make so long as it wasn't a rubber dingy with leaks?

If you had grown up two thousand kilometres from any ocean, had never before been afloat and were not sure if you knew how to swim, it was essential to put your trust in God, Lord of the worlds.

He remembered something Monsieur Bruno had said. Almost every species of mammal could swim if pursued by a fierce enough predator, even if water was not their natural habitat.

Hands Across the Sea

While resting on the cool floor, she observed her boy, busy with his flags and posters. It was good for a child on whom inactivity had been forced to have an absorbing hobby. She must imitate his sense of purpose. She began to arrange her own possessions, the books, journals, ring-files, lining them up on a shelf, with a jar of sharpened pencils and computer discs, waiting to be filled with the fruits of her research.

She so hoped it would be a profitable stay, in all respects. 'It really is a pleasing apartment,' she said. 'N'est ce pas?'

'Oui.'

'Bigger than we might have expected.'

'Yes, Maman.' He couldn't work out which language they were supposed to be using.

'Scholars don't usually have dependants with them.'

'Oui. Je le sais.'

'How do you know it?'

'There were two of them downstairs. By the cars. One of them was surprised about me.'

'Naturally you will have to go to school.'

'Je le sais, Maman. Of course.'

'You won't mind, will you? Attending school? While I am in the library?'

He said, '*I* wouldn't want to sit in a library all day. You know that.' He was planning on being outside whenever he could for he'd identified the white rocks round here. Limestone. Calcium carbonate. First rate for the novice fossil hunter. Flags and posters had palled. It was time for the change. If he found a fossil, even one lowly ammonite, he'd have the theme to launch a new collection.

Rules of the Game

For the Scholars' Orientation Meeting, she put on the grey suit she wore for parents' evening at Jebb's. He hated those meetings. Often, an attack prevented him from attending. Here was different. He knew he must go, to look after her because she was so nervous.

They crossed the tropical gardens which whirred with evening insects. They entered the main building. They sidled into the Grande Salle. The other Scholars were already there. Twelve of them. He knew they must all be clever, at least as clever as Anne-Marie who didn't even know how to scramble an egg.

At the sight of them, she clutched his hand in a panic. 'Ah non! Non, non, non. Mon Dieu! Look, look at me. It is all wrong!'

Was it being the thirteenth Scholar that worried her?

He said, 'It'll be okay. I'm here too. I make it fourteen.'

But it wasn't superstition over being thirteenth. It

was how she was dressed, in her formal grey suit. The other twelve were in flowery Hawaiians and gaudy Bermudas.

He made her sit down just behind the others. 'Maman, you look fine.' He kept hold of her hand to make sure she stayed.

The meeting was as draggy as anything at Jebb's. The director's welcome speech was long and repetitive. Regulations of the Institut. Responsibilities, requirements, duties and commitments of the Scholars.

Hamish concentrated on the International Maritime Signalling Code. He remembered that the flag conveying the message I AM ON FIRE AND HAVE DANGEROUS CARGO ON BOARD KEEP WELL CLEAR OF ME was a simple design. But was it the one with the blue background and the white stripe, or the red background? If he were commander of a burning vessel, it would make the difference between life and death of his crew that he selected the correct flag. Another query. What constituted 'dangerous' cargo? Could it mean live alligators, drums of nuclear waste, or psychotic killers being transported to an island fortress? He decided there and then that a life at sea would not do for him. It would be too risky, especially as he couldn't swim very well. The chlorine at the pool they went to from Jebb's used to affect his breathing. The sports teacher had told him not to come any more. He was a liability.

The director was rounding off his talk. He had white hair, pink cheeks and spoke in English. 'So, in conclusion, I urge each and every one of you to profit from your semester here in our asylum of academic peace. And I mean all.' He fixed his pale eyes on Hamish.

Hamish squirmed. Why bring him into it? He was only here to look after Anne-Marie.

'I want also to welcome the youngest member of our circle. Although he is not a Scholar, he is as much a part of this community as any. Yes, boy, I mean you.' The scary eyes glittered. 'You understand my meaning?'

Why hadn't he stayed safely up in the apartment? Anne-Marie was nudging him. She whispered, 'Dr Whyte is expecting a response.'

'Yes,' Hamish said aloud.

Anne-Marie nudged him again. 'Sir,' she prompted in a whisper.

'Yes, sir,' he said.

'So let us begin as we mean to go on, heh?'

'Yes, sir.'

'So there will be no running amok, heh?'

'Yes, sir.'

'The library is out of bounds unless in the company of an adult.'

Why would I *want* to go in a library full of books on medieval French history? 'Yes, sir.'

'The rules intended for Scholars apply also to you. And under no circumstances are you to make use of the photocopier in the computer room. And no nonsense on the banisters, heh? We all know what a temptation a long banister is to a young chap. We will nip unsocial behaviour in the bud before it takes root, heh?'

'Yes, sir. Thank you, sir.'

Apéritifs du Soir

The Scholars were gathering outside the building. They were to go down into the village, portside, they said, for celebratory drinks. 'We gotta check out the local appellation.'

'Taste the local brew.'

'Experience the Gallic ambience.'

'Get to know one another. Mingle and fraternize.'

They were inviting Anne-Marie to go with them. She dithered, shyly, using Hamish as her excuse. 'I cannot leave my son hon 'is first night.'

'Hey, c'mon! Loosen up, ma'am. The kid comes too. We're family!'

Suddenly, Hamish found himself picked up and flung over a man's shoulder in a firefighter's lift. His carrier was Ned, the big American. He set off at a gallop towards the village, whooping like a cowboy.

'You okay up there, Homer?' he called out.

Hamish didn't know. Nobody had ever carried him

like this before. He wasn't convinced it was fun, jolting rapidly downhill, upside down, seeing nothing but the steep stone steps underneath his head and a pair of suntanned feet, running. He became scared. What if they reached the waterfront and Ned couldn't stop? They'd both go in. Hamish wasn't much of a swimmer.

When he was frightened, his throat constricted.

They reached the quayside. Ned set him gently down. Hamish staggered, giddy and gasping. His throat began making the embarrassing chicken noise. Ned held on to him with a secure grip.

'Take it easy, son,' Ned said. 'Didn't mean to give you the heebie-jeebies.'

The panic passed. The air went in and out of the lungs as it should.

'You okay? Ready to join the gang?'

They had already settled into the Peroquet Bleu. Dishes of olives, pickled cauliflower and gherkins came with their drinks. They'd got him a glass of something coloured orange. If it had any of the Es in it, it'd restart the wheezing. He sipped. It turned out to be juice, nice and pure. Even the gherkins didn't taste so bad.

'Say Annie, what's yours? Beer, wine, pastis?'

They'd misheard her name. They were calling her Annie. They called Hamish Homer. Hamish protested. 'I haven't got a flat voice or a brown muzzle.'

'No, not *that* Homer.'

'The real one. The poet. Greek.'

Ned, seeing his bewilderment, provided a brief explication of *The Odyssey*. Then they were chatting together as if they'd known each other all their lives though none had met before today. They drew Anne-Marie into their talk of bursaries, projects, doctorates, colloquiums.

Then they talked about where their ancestors had originated from. Two had Irish forefathers. One had relatives still living in Sicily. Another had grandparents who'd emigrated from Dundee.

'Gee, that is such a wonderful country, Scotland. I been back to trace the family.'

There was a Pole, a German, another whose parents had crossed into USA from Canada, and before that had crossed the Pacific from Vietnam. Yet they were also Americans. They had unity with difference. Proud to be Americans, proud to be from elsewhere.

Anne-Marie wasn't volunteering anything. Nobody pressed her. Ned asked Hamish, 'So hows about you, Homer?' He pronounced it 'Omer. 'Where do you hail from?'

The waiter returned with more drinks and another dish of snacks. This time, green olives and cubes of dark red sausage.

'That's tapas,' said Ned. 'Spanish. Taste it.'

Hamish tried the sausage. The fatty spicy flavour flooded him with a memory of Douglas extolling the virtues of McFadyen's black puddings. Then he seemed to hear him say, Think on William Wallace. Our thinkers are more innovative. Who invented the British Broadcasting Corporation, world renowned for authority and dependability? Come on, lad, hazard a guess.

Er, could it have been a Scot?

'Aye indeed it was so. One John Reith by name, place of birth Stonehaven. Aberdeenshire.'

'So tell us then, 'Omer, where are *you* from?'

He wanted them to like him, especially big Ned. He wanted intriguingly complex roots like they had. Greater London, with its nonexistent Turks, pen-stealers, car-thieves and mother-abductors was banal. He'd left all that behind. To come from Greater London was to admit to being an insignificant speck among seven million, two hundred and eight-five thousand other Greater Londoners.

Hamish took a gulp of Orangina. 'Scotland,' he said softly, in what he thought was a good imitation of Douglas's voice.

Anne-Marie glanced at him with raised eyebrows. He avoided her eye.

'Aye, ma roots are in Scotland,' he added more confidently. Douglas would prove his worth.

The Neo-Scot

It is strange, the wealth of knowledge one can recall when in sudden need. Information to which one has formerly closed one's ears. And here it all was, pre-packed inside his head for foreign travel.

He embraced, with enthusiasm, the heritage that was not his.

The captivating folklore with its boggarts and kelpies, the history of courage, the Years of Enlightenment second to none, the Industrial Revolution that rivalled England's in speed and scope. Ship-building, iron smelting, textiles and woollens.

'The Forth Bridge is the second longest cantilever bridge in the whole world. The reason there are no Roman amphitheatres, triumphal arches or long, straight roads in Scotland is because the Romans never ever managed to get the better of the Scots. Without Robbie Burns there'd be no Auld Lang Syne for the world's party-goers on New Year's Eve.'

Did the melting-pot Scholars, listening so attentively, believe any of this?

He must have got some of it right because nobody contradicted him, though Anne-Marie stared. Then the Scholar with the Dundee roots asked, 'Do you know anything of Uist?'

Uist. Was it bird, weaponry, Gaelic foodstuff, castle? He scrabbled in his database for relevant info. He found nothing. Stick with the resolve: strong, heroic, imaginative.

'Not yet,' he replied pensively. 'Gie me time. I'm no wee sleekit cow'rin mousie but I'm still nae more than a laddie. I haven't seen everything yet.'

And they all laughed, kindly.

Anne-Marie and the Metamorphosis

Had they been here seven weeks, seven months or just seven days? The nearness of the sea, the brightness of the sun, the shininess of the stars made time behave erratically.

He heard her wake, humming. She was always humming. He heard her unlatch the wooden shutters and throw them open and gasp. She gasped every time she looked out.

'Oh chéri, bonjour! Do come here to see!' she called like a trilling bird. 'The sun, it is just rising over the cliff. So beautiful!'

He pulled on his tee-shirt with scarcely a wheeze. It used to take ten minutes on the nebulizer to start the day. Now, just a little light coughing. He joined her on the balcony. He gazed down into the water. It changed, constantly. This morning, deep blue with paler stripes where the breeze ruffled the surface. He could see a shoal of fish shimmering.

She said, 'Did you know we are in paradise? And we do not deserve all this.'

What did she mean? 'Of course we do.' They'd had those really bad times. And now, thanks to their own inner strength, they'd come through. They deserved anything decent that came their way. Some famous guy had said something like that: Suffer and you shall receive your recompense. And they had.

She brought two bowls of drinking chocolate and a basket of croissants on to the balcony. 'It does seem too good to be real, doesn't it?' she said. 'An enchanted place which I never expected to exist.'

He dipped his croissant into the chocolate and squinted out to sea. From up here, he could watch every vessel that made its way into or out of harbour. Right now, three fishing boats, blue and white, chugging out. The man at the tiller of the leading craft greeted them with a wave. 'Bonjour. Bon appétit!' Later, there'd be the pleasure yachts, speedboats, ferries, catamarans, small cruise liners, heading in for the marina. He observed. He jotted down their flags in his spiral notebook.

She too, was listing good things. 'Primo. Freedom from pressures and worry.'

'Oui Maman.'

'Secondo. Institut personnel staff, always helpful.'

'Oui, Maman.'

'Oh 'Amish, do you see this clarity of the light! It is so stupefying!'

'Oui.'

'And sis beautiful sea 'oo is stretching so far to the horizon.' When emotional, she slid, unaware, from one language to the other. She had no primary tongue. She hadn't much clue who she was, where she belonged. She'd wanted him to learn one of her childhood languages to bolster up her own identity.

'The library 'ere which is so satisfying to me. Also the chief librarian. He shows such good will.'

In which language should he respond to her soupy monologues? It became easy when he realized that she couldn't tell the difference.

'Oui Maman. C'est important.'

'And Les Mimosas, it is so spacious, so airy.' She was back with the French. 'The affability of the Scholars. The charm of the village. It is not like the people of the north. This cheerfulness, candidness of local people. But oh Hamish, mon chéri, I am thinking only of myself. I should be thinking of you. Is it good for you too?'

There was only one answer she wanted. 'Oui Maman. C'est magnifique. I am glad we came. Just one thing, why do you let them call you Annie? It has never

145

been your name. You must make them get it right.'

A nonchalant shrug. 'So why? I like this Annie. She suits me.'

The new Annie smiled more than Anne-Marie. She laughed. She dressed differently. She *was* different. Annie tied a pink head-scarf round her hair, then flounced it up to make it big like a butterfly. Annie folded Anne-Marie's grey suit back into the case and slid it under the bed. Annie wore bright tee-shirts and a cotton skirt she'd found in the market, patterned with sunflowers and cicadas. Annie looked like the merry goose-girl in the picture book that the grandmother had read to Hamish, the Scot, a long time ago.

'Okay, keep the name, so long as it makes you happy.'

He liked her better when she was happy.

Embarcation for the Land of Hope

On a distant shore, by the light of the silvery moon, a little wooden boat slipped out to sea. It was riding low. On board were the captain, his mate, sixteen men and one boy, a heavier cargo than the vessel was designed to carry. Normally, it held red mullet, John Dory, Dakar sole and sardines, none of which cared how they were handled once they'd stopped gasping. Travelling men took up more space, but at a higher profit.

Some might think that a moonlit night was no time to set out on a clandestine voyage. But the skipper had paid the necessary sweetner to the harbourmaster so that, moon or no moon, blind eyes would turn in any direction and see nothing that shouldn't be there.

There was not space for all to be seated at the same time. They took turns to perch on the gunwales, took turns to stand. The eldest passenger, father of the boy, was the only voyager who could not take his turn standing. He lay in the bows as unaware of his surroundings as a sardine and taking up as much space as five men. The skipper noticed that he had a bad smell. He knew he should never have let him aboard.

What he didn't know was that the man had previously had an infected leg wound. To prevent the gangrene taking further hold, the leg had been removed by an unlicensed surgeon at the port. The spread of gangrene had not been halted. The site of the amputation was festering.

Even though both his father and his uncle were there, the boy was deeply afraid; but not as afraid as he had been in the warehouse.

Nobody spoke on the rocking boat, except for the occasional command from the skipper to his mate, in a language which the boy didn't recognize.

When the uncle felt his nephew shivering, he asked, 'Faisal, are you afraid?'

Faisal was not the boy's name. It was the name printed inside the travel document that had been bought for him. The uncle had to get him accustomed to the new name. When they arrived on the far side, there must be no possible cause for suspicion from anyone in authority.

The small picture pasted and laminated inside the document was of a stranger. This boy Faisal would have to get used to a changed identity.

He shook his head. 'No, not afraid. Just cold. This jacket is not thick.' He didn't want his uncle to think him a coward.

'I am never cold. Here. You take this.' The uncle took off his jacket and gave it to his nephew. 'It is a warm night. We are blessed.'

The loan of the jacket was to save the boy's life. It is often thought that drowned people have died from water inhalation. In fact, just as often, their death is from hypothermia well before water has entered their lungs.

The boy heard his uncle search for a cigarette and heard the strike of the match on the box, and he saw the tiny yellow flare of flame. His uncle said gently, 'There is no need for any of us to be afraid. The difficulties of the journey are over. Now we submit to the divinity. Tomorrow we will begin our new life.'

The boy saw the red dot in the darkness of the lighted cigarette glow brighter as it was inhaled, then move like a firefly as it was passed from one hand to the next. When the boat moved out into choppier water, this time-passing activity ceased. A vertical traveller needed both hands to keep himself steady.

Yves and le Rosbif

When a person lives in an agreeable apartment, with an agreeable view and an agreeable climate, he can think agreeable thoughts. Agreeability multiplies like the daisies in a verdant lawn.

All aspects of Hamish's life were becoming agreeable. When he was with the Scholars, especially Ned, Hamish felt enfolded in affection. It was like gaining an elder brother.

Even starting at his new school was no ordeal. The bus pick-up point was beside the big white rock opposite the Institute gates. Another boy was already waiting.

Hamish nodded, smiled. 'Bonjour,' he said. He kept his right hand ready inside his jacket. He was unsure whether French boys of his age shook hands as the adults all did.

The other boy nodded curtly. 'Salut,' he said. No hand-shake required.

When Hamish climbed on board, did the other pupils lob books at him? Pocket his pens? Appropriate his sports gear? Practise their slicing-the-bacon technique on his ears? They did not. They welcomed him, made a place for him to sit. They clustered round, eager and genial.

'Good morning,' they said.

'Goodbye.'

'What time is it?'

'What is the weather today?'

'Where is Buckingham Palace?'

'My name is Pierre.'

'My name is Luc (or Louis or Michel). What is your name?'

In the class to which Hamish was allocated, the boys were eager to practise their stock phrases. None mocked Hamish's own careful way of speaking their language, as pupils at Eglantine Jebb had mocked each foreign newcomer.

Hamish had anticipated that his peers would find 'Hamish' as difficult to pronounce as Anne-Marie did. So he told them that, in French, Hamish was Henri.

One boy refuted this. 'Rosbif is your name! Everybody knows. The perfidious Albion is always called le Rosbif.' It was Yves, who had boarded the bus at the same place as Hamish.

151

Pierre whispered, 'He is the son of the mayor. And his father's a member of the Rotarians.'

Hamish didn't mind being called the roast-beef. There were worse insults at Jebb's. But Yves had been overheard by one of the pions who stalked the recreation yard like secret agents. Back at Jebb's they called them prefects.

The son of the mayor was told by the pion to apologize which, to Hamish's bewilderment, he did.

Smiling, open-face, right hand outstretched, Yves approached him at the end of the day. 'Excuse me. I regret my action. I intended it only in fun. So listen, do not go back on the bus. Come with me. My father is picking me up in the cabriolet. It's my tennis coaching today. Perhaps you'd like to come and play me one day soon. You live with the Americans, don't you? We're in the red villa just behind.'

So at the end of his first school day, Hamish found himself being shown on to the back seat of an open-top car. Yves's father, at the wheel, said, 'So you are the new American lad?'

'New, monsieur, yes. But also no. Not from the States. From Scotland.'

'Ahah,' the mayor said. 'And in Edinburgh I have tried your special porridge as you call it. Very curious victuals. Oatmeal soup, is it not?'

'Oui, monsieur.'

Yves, sitting beside his father in the front, giggled.

The mayor had a suntanned face, with crinkly smile and shiny raven-black hair. He reminded Hamish of the film star on his The Wages of Fear poster.

The mayor took a different route from the bus. He was offering a speed-tour of significant local sights. The war memorial, the marina, the Mairie with the tricolor flag flying where he had his mayorial suite, the famous Fishery Tribunal and historic Harbourmaster's House, the public bathing beach fringed by palm trees imported from Mauritius, dotted with parasols from Martinique.

'We import the sand too,' the mayor informed Hamish over his shoulder.

'You should see it in high summer,' said Yves, turning right round from the front passenger seat. 'Packed! We go to the Pyrénées in August, don't we Papa?'

For the next sight, they roared out of the village and up the zigzag road to the yellow church perched on the big rock. The father stopped at a viewing point.

'Voilà!' He spread his arms to encompass the panorama of sea and hills as if it all were his. He obviously considered himself the most important person around. Douglas used to have a phrase for men like that, the heid bummer.

'Pretty place, heh, jeune homme? The Mediterranean's best-kept secret, as we call it in the guide-book.'

He pointed out the Italianate palazzo on the promontory where some famous opera singer that Hamish had never heard of lived, the restored fourteenth-century hermit's chapel on the end of the further peninsula, the remains of the Napoleonic fortress on the point.

'And before they built that lighthouse on the headland, sailors relied on this sacred building as their navigational aid. The village kept a lamp on the tower so sailors could steer a safe course. Our people have always earned their living from the sea. So they've always lent a helping hand to other seafarers. It's the way we are, generous hearted.'

He smiled, showing his teeth, which were as unusually white as the hair and moustache were evenly black. If he dyed his hair, perhaps he bleached his teeth too.

Next, they went revving off past the luxury residencies clinging to the hillside. Each had its own azure pool. The terraced gardens spilled over with red, purple, orange flowers, bright as Hawaiian shirts. Then through vineyards. Hamish felt the warm, scented air blowing past his face. If only Anne-Marie's ramshackle car could have an open top like this.

They turned off the road and on to a bumpy track. 'Short cut,' said the mayor. 'Takes us direct to the corniche, the finest sight of all.'

They swooped on to a road running high above the sapphire sea. 'C'est magnifique, heh?'

The most disturbing local sight wasn't pointed out at all, though Hamish spotted it as they passed.

Shacksville in Arcadia

'What's that, down there?' he asked.

The road ran alongside a deep chasm, the kind of unexpected hole in the ground that a falling meteorite might have created, except this appeared man-made, for the sides and base were smooth.

'That was the old quarry. Where they used to cut the limestone.'

'And what's down there now?'

The mayor went on with an explanation of stone-cutting, as if he hadn't heard. 'All the older houses of the village are built from the same stone. And the church of course. But they ceased quarrying here thirty years or more ago.'

Hamish could make out a cluster of huts at the bottom of the quarry, huddled against the wall, and some leaning against each other for support. A few had tin roofs with thin chimneys sticking up. Most had plastic sheets for roofs, held down with stones, or were patched with strips of wood. Some appeared to be made entirely from cardboard packing cases.

'So who lives there?'

The mayor waved his hand to point out another local feature. 'Out there, is what we call the garrigue. Wild country.' He was deliberately distracting Hamish from the quarry. 'Good hunting up there in the right season.'

'Hunting?' said Hamish.

'Shooting,' said the mayor. 'Just for sport.' He half turned and smiled the easy smile which showed all the gleaming teeth. 'Men round here are good at many sports. At the correct season of year, they like to shoot. Bécasse, cul-blanc, grive.'

Hamish didn't know these words. What could these creatures be that the men went out to hunt? Wild boar? Stags? Hares? 'Grive?' he queried.

'Oui, grive musicienne.' The mayor whistled a couple of bird-like notes. 'In English you call him, singing thrush.'

Wasn't a thrush that garden bird the RSPB told you to feed in wintertime? Hamish said, 'You shoot little birds?'

The mayor laughed. 'Better than the American sport of shooting men in the street, heh? Like in Los Angeles?'

Hamish said, 'So who's in the huts down there?'

'Nobody,' said the mayor. 'Nobody lives there.'

Why would he say that when the place looked inhabited? Hamish was sure he'd seen smoke coming from a stovepipe chimney.

'Not any more.'

Hamish had definitely seen a pair of trousers hanging on a washing line.

'I admit, a few years back we had a bit of trouble with migrants squatting, creating themselves a bidonville. They came over here to labour for us, all legal, but when their time was up, they wouldn't go. They tried to stay. Not like the labourers in my great-grandfather's time. Things were different then. They had immigrant workers from all over. Vietnamese and Chinese mostly, invited over to build the new steam railway, Paris to Nice. An engineering feat.'

Hamish felt Yves's father was deliberately changing direction.

'There was the Promenade des Anglais further along, at Nice, Englishman saw to the building of that. Artist, he was. Funny chap. Had fits, so my arrière-grandfather told my arrière-grandmother. So with the Promenade des Anglais, they needed a railway to get them here. No motorways then. So these chinks came and worked like blacks. Splendid chaps they must have been.'

Yves yawned with a wide open mouth to demonstrate his boredom with a lecture he'd heard before.

His father carried on regardless. 'And when they'd done the job, they trotted home to their wives and families. None of them stayed more than ten years. Well, so maybe one or two overstayed their welcome, but not so you'd notice. Not like these modern men. Africans for the most part, North Africans. Come and do the jobs they're asked to then think they can stay for ever. Start shipping in their wives, children, cousins, brothers, grandmothers, second wives. They'll have any number of wives, those musulmans, ha ha ha. Well, we don't tolerate that sort of behaviour here. This is a decent place, decent and pleasant. Secluded and special. And that's the way we're going to keep it.'

They were drawing up in front of the Institute gates, a halfway-round-the-world trip in less than twenty minutes.

The mayor held out his hand to say goodbye.

'Merci, monsieur,' said Hamish.

'Our pleasure. To show our visitor from Scotland that we too have many beautiful places. So maybe you will come and sail with us one weekend? There is a little creek we sometimes go to. They do oysters and an excellent salade niçoise. Yves would appreciate your company and he might bother to pick up a little English. Though he is a lazy boy, aren't you?'

The following day in school was not so agreeable. Yves informed the class that the Scottish boy's real name was Mister Porridge.

Hamish said, 'Porridge is not a name! You heard your father. It is something we eat.'

Yves said, 'Yes. It is oatmeal soup. If you don't care for Porridge, perhaps you prefer Oatmeal? It's amusing.'

Hamish must keep his annoyance under control. The chance of tennis and sailing was too good to relinquish. More profitable to keep Yves as pal than enemy. If Yves insisted on calling him Oatmeal, he wouldn't complain. He must remain resolute in his strength, heroism and imagination. Imaginatively, he revealed to Yves the identity of one of his ancestors.

'William Wallace,' he said. '*Sir* William Wallace.' The Republican French had a deep fascination for titled aristocracy, so Douglas had claimed.

But Yves had never heard of Scotland's national hero and wasn't impressed, even when Hamish explained that Wallace had been sheltered by the French when fleeing from the perfidious English. 'In the film,' Hamish persisted, 'they called him Braveheart.'

Still no positive reaction, just more Oatmeal, Oatmeal.

'He had a big sword,' Hamish went on. 'Killed loads of his enemies. These days, we do sword-fighting at school in honour of the great courage he showed on the field of battle.'

Yves looked at him doubtfully. Hamish wondered, Was he pushing Yves's credulity too far? One more try. 'And he wore blue skin-dye, which we call woad.'

The blue war-paint was the trigger. Yves had, after all, heard of the wild warrior.

'I have a picture of him,' Hamish said. 'On one of my classic film posters. You could come over and see my collection, any time.'

Yves said, 'Sure, Oatmeal Soup Porridge. But not this weekend. I will be crewing for my uncle. We have to go to Ventimiglia.'

'Oh. Right. Ventimiglia.' Wherever that might be. As obscure as Uist. Next door to Uist, for all Hamish knew.

'We have to fetch over six aunts. And the cousins. And Mémé. It's the old lady's birthday. Father says my grandmother enjoys coming by water. It's faster than the motorway. Always such congestion above Nice, isn't there?'

'Oui.'

'Tourists, Father says. Germans, mostly. You know what Germans are like. The Belgians aren't so bad. I'd invite you too, Porridge, but there's already over a hundred guests. My mother would have a fit. Anyhow, it won't be much fun. You know how these big family occasions are. Bit of an ordeal.'

'Yes. Big family get-togethers,' agreed Hamish. 'Nightmare time.' As if he had any idea. Him and old uncle Wallace, celebrating with their woad and oatmeal soup, as was their wont.

Travel Sickness

The boy who did not look nor feel like Faisal saw the sun rise over the rim of the world. He saw his uncle bend and dip his hand to the sea to take up some drops of water with which to purify himself for the Soobh Fegr. He saw his uncle turn and his lips move and he understood what his uncle was saying. 'Praise be to God, Lord of the worlds.'

To the west the boy saw a bank of cloud clinging to a new coast. It had to be the edge of Europe. He felt a surge of excitement and relief. Soon, this perpetual motion would end. But to his disappointment, the boat wasn't making for land. It chugged on into the vast spaces of open sea. When the burning sun was at its height, the boy was overcome with an intense moment of despair that the world could be so huge and that he and his companions were such insignificant specks on its surface.

The men passed round the drinking water. The sun

went down. They passed the flat bread and dates. The old man could not eat his share. The uncle managed to get him to take a sip of water. But he didn't speak. At dusk he became delirious, babbling gibberish. He didn't seem like a man who used to be the head of his family. His face was hollow. He looked like a spectre. Just after nightfall, he stopped moving. The uncle bent over him and whispered for him the sacred words, 'la ilah illa Allah wa Muhammad rasul Allah,' and the boy who was not Faisal knew that his father was on the point of death. When the uncle put his ear close to the body and listened, the boy knew his father had died.

The skipper was an infidel and looked angry when he realized. He shouted and gestured in a way that indicated clearly, 'Get rid of him!'

The old man was rolled in his blanket. He was lifted over the gunwales and slid into the water. The boy watched but didn't help. His uncle held his shoulder and pressed hard. The boy did not cry lest he shame his uncle or anger the captain.

Sweet Pastry,
Sweet Life

He was down from the bus, through the automatic gates. White afternoon sun bounced off the walls of the Institut. It felt like home. He passed one of the women in her blue apron, polishing the entrance hall on hands and knees. She moved aside to let him pass.

'Bonsoir, young man,' she said.

'Bonsoir, madame,' he replied. Halfway up the stairway, he deliberately let slip his schoolbag from his hold. He wanted to see what would happen. The servant picked it up and followed up the steps to hand it to him.

'Voilà!' she said.

'Merci, madame,' he said.

So now he knew what servants did. They took care of you. It felt good. He let himself into Les Mimosas. The apartment was shadowy and he could hear the swish of the waves. It smelled of the eau de Javel they used for cleaning the tiles. The servant had been in here too.

Anne-Marie was still over in the library. She took her studying seriously. Nobody was forcing her. She followed her own agenda. She did it because she wanted to.

He pushed open the louvered shutters and let in light. Below, the waxy palms shimmered. The strange blossoms smouldered. The indigo waves danced. A catamaran boogied out to sea.

Homework was supposed to take one hour. Even an idiot could manage it. Were he to do it incorrectly, the teachers would make allowances. Being a foreigner had some advantages. He finished it in twenty minutes, checked it, then pocketed the twenty-euro note Anne-Marie had left out for him and went in search of their supper. Here, it didn't matter a jot that she could scarcely boil an egg satisfactorily. In the village, there was fresh fish, dried fish, marinated fish, shellfish. On Friday evenings sardines were grilled by the trayful on the jetty. In the épicerie he could find pâtés and strange stinky cheeses wrapped in brown leaves or rolled in wood-ash, pies and fougasse. In the market on Wednesdays were melons and figs, olives and sour-sweet gherkins. He was growing to love their special taste.

He trotted down the steps and headed first for the bakery. The boulanger fired up the oven at four in the morning, at eleven, and again at four in the afternoon. The people expected their bread to be fresh for each meal.

'Bonsoir, madame,' said Hamish to the baker's wife. He appreciated the formality of life here. You knew where you were, so long as you said the correct things at the correct time.

'And bonsoir to you, young man,' she said. 'Hasn't it been a lovely day and how are you settling in?'

'Merci, madame. Very well,' said Hamish. 'It is very good here. One baguette, please. And two portions of pizza, if you please, one with olives and one with anchovy.'

'Aha, so you like our anchovies, jeune homme?'

'Oui, madame. Your anchovies are very good. Merci.'

She handed him the loaf in a twist of tissue paper, the pizza slices folded into greaseproof paper, and a fresh-fruit pastry which she'd wrapped into a little parcel and tied with red string.

Hamish was perplexed. 'Non, madame,' he said. 'I didn't order the pastry.'

She laughed. 'And I offer it to you, jeune homme. We all hope you will be very happy during your stay here. It is good that young people from all over visit us.

And when you return to your country you will tell them what a good life it is here.'

'Oui, madame. Merci, madame,' said Hamish as he paid for the baguette and the pizza but not for the pastry. Every addition sum that he did in his head, counting the figures in French, was another step forward in Calcul. He remembered to say 'Bonsoir, madame' and 'Au revoir, madame' and 'Till tomorrow, madame,' and, as he left the bakery he heard Madame inform the next customer what a pleasant young man he was, that he was from Sweden, or possibly Holland. But definitely not one of the Americans.

It was reassuring to know he was a pleasant person. He sauntered along the waterfront and heard music that made his feet want to skip. He saw a man at the Café Danube playing the accordion. An elderly woman rose from another table, crossed to the man, placed her hands on the back of his chair to steady herself and began to sing.

Hamish had heard buskers at the entrance to the Underground, grubby, grungy boys who gave you the evil eye when you put nothing in the greasy hat on the pavement in front of them. But these weren't buskers. There was no hat. They weren't asking for money. They were making music for happiness's sake.

He hopped and skipped up sixty-three steps without

a pause. He did not pant. Here, there was no asthma. Nor were there buskers or beggars or inkies or addicts. No rubbish piled up on the steps. Instead, growing out of a crack in the rock was a tropical succulent with oval leaves and orange flowers. There were so many things here that he'd never seen before. He loved them all.

On the sixty-fourth step he paused to look back and admire.

He set the table. Two places. Him and her, side by side, looking out over their balcony. So compact a family. He prepared a bowl of coloured salad leaves, burgundy red, plum purple, jade green. The stall-holder had thrown in a handful of marigold heads as well.

'Delicious!' she had said. 'Put them in your salad. Rejuvenating and appetizing!'

With care, he unwrapped his pastry. It was mille-feuille, layered with raspberries, strawberries and crème anglaise, frosted with fine sucre patissier. How he had changed. A year ago, he would have taken such a gift to his room to consume alone. Now, he would share it. He sliced it into two equal portions. Everything was ready for the return of his family.

He breathed calmly in time with the slip-slap of the water. He watched the scarlet sunset and the pale-blue dusk compete for control. Night was winning. He saw the lights twinkling round the harbour. This was the real world. That other place, with its riots, tear-gas, noise, overcrowding and stress, was the false one.

Venus, the twilight star, glittered like tinsel. The first of the evening cruise-liners made its stately way along the horizon. Another followed, like a spangled circus elephant. The big liners were crisscrossing the sea from Casablanca to La Ciotat, from Tangiers to Toulon, Genoa to Ajaccio, Palermo to Naples, Marseille to Malaga, La Spezia to Palma. But not here. The harbour was too shallow to receive them. And that was how the mayor wished it to remain. Yves said, 'Papa says we wouldn't want them. They carry the wrong type of tourists. We have to maintain the status quo. We do not want the peace disrupted.'

On Sunday week he'd be sailing with Yves. The week after, he was going to meet up with Yves for tennis after school. This existence was first class. And went on getting better. Hamish understood, for the first time, that the point of life was for living, just for the living and the laughing and the having fun. That was all there was to it. He'd come to the place where they'd cracked the code.

But the Scholars' bursaries were only for two semesters, half a year. He must find a means of ensuring they stayed forever. He'd once thought he didn't care where he lived. But now he knew.

He heard the clang of the gates. Then the click of the main door and the pitter-patter of her feet on the marble stairs. She was on her way home. When she came back, her eyes tired from poring over her manuscripts, her wrists aching from tapping on the keyboard, she would always ask him straightaway about his day. He would tell her all the good things. He would tell her how he wanted them to stay here forever.

Then the storms brewed up from the middle of the pretty sea and smashed up a Scots boy's Utopian fancies. That was before the first of the bodies began to wash up on the rocks.

Access Denied

The men were already drained from the insecurity they'd experienced, waiting to depart. Now came further uncertainty about the likely outcome of their trip. They had paid the unknown intermediary in the good faith that they would be conveyed to a European port. They had not been able to state their destination preference, but had been led to believe it was more likely to be Gibraltar than Lampedusa. But every aspect of the voyage was down to chance. Safe, speedy travel was never part of the deal. The disposition of the captain, the expertise of his seamanship, the seaworthiness of his craft, were all the luck of the draw.

The boy who might once have been Ahmed, and soon would be Faisal, understood this. The decisions had been made by the adults. He could see how they were losing confidence in the skipper, who was becoming increasingly irritable, snapping at his helmsman as well as at the nervous cargo. He ordered the passengers each to take a turn on watch duty. The boy too.

At dawn, when the skipper dozed upright on the gunwales, wedged between two passengers, it was the boy who was first to spot the sliver of coastline to the west. The helmsman made for it. It glowed golden in the sunrise. The boy could hardly wait to reach the calm water of a harbour, and to step out onto solid land. A launch was speeding out to meet them. This would be the Red Cross reception committee that his father had said would help them.

But they were the coastguards. They were shouting instructions through a loud-hailer. The skipper did not proclaim his captaincy. Quite the reverse. He squatted down in the bows with his jacket over his head.

The boy understood. He told his uncle, 'These are coastguards and they say it is prohibited to stop here. If any of us attempts to come ashore we will be arrested and deported the same day.'

His uncle said, 'Beg them to be merciful. Tell them one of us has already died on this journey.'

The boy did as he was told. The official in the prow of the launch shouted, 'Do you require water?'

The boy didn't consult his uncle. On his own initiative, he called back, 'Yes! Water! And also food!'

A twenty-five-litre plastic cubitainer of drinking water, but no food, was swung over. The wooden boat was attached to the aft of the launch and towed back out to sea where the towing rope was untied. One of the travellers tried to throw himself overboard but was held back by two of his compatriots.

The skipper had done the trip five times before. Never a problem, always a profit. These men were jinxing his boat. This was the first time he'd had a death on board. They'd known the old fellow was sick. He had a good mind to tip them all overboard. Nobody would ever know. But he was outnumbered. He might end up in the water himself.

Anxiety made him angrier. He screamed at the men, 'I hate you asylum seekers. This trip is endangering my life, my livelihood, my family's future. Why should I risk all that I have for you scum? You must pay me more.'

One said haltingly, 'We have no more.'

'You are all liars. You have more. What were you going to do when you arrived? Stand in the street and beg? I know you have money hidden.'

He was right. Three men fumbled with the linings of their tunics, the turn-ups of their caps, the heel of their shoes and produced money. The boy wondered if his father had gone overboard with their emergency fund still in his belt or if his uncle had managed to retrieve it without being seen. He wanted to ask but couldn't risk the others hearing. The captain again asked each man in turn if they had more money. When the boy's uncle shook his head, the nephew had no idea whether to believe him.

They carried on through the middle of the day, keeping the dull smudge of coastline within sight, without themselves being spotted. Misty rain gathered and camouflaged them. Their luck was changing.

But the captain knew the situation was still too risky to attempt a landing. He decided to get them within reasonable distance of the shore before ordering them to leave. Then they'd stand a chance. As dusk fell, he steered landward through low cloud, towards a stretch of scrubby coast which appeared to be uninhabited.

Appearances can be deceptive. To everybody's surprise and terror, they found themselves being fired on from sentry posts hidden along the coast. Warning shots, so nobody was hurt but the message was clear. The fishing boat headed out to sea once again.

In Paradise Fishes
and Angels Swim

On Sunday, when Yves would be ferrying numerous relatives to a family party, Hamish reclassified his flags and Anne-Marie read. An enthusiastic rap at the door of Les Mimosas startled them. Hamish went to the door. It was Ned, in walking-boots and baseball cap.

'Hi, 'Omer.'

'Bonjour,' said Hamish. It was time Ned made an effort with his French.

'Your mom home? I've a great idea for a hike. I've discovered this hidden cove. She's going to go ape when I show her. It's just crazy. Will you go ask her?'

So Hamish asked. And Anne-Marie wasn't pleased. 'Chéri, please tell him we are busy.'

Hamish said to Ned, 'She's uncovered an important new seam of significant information. She's mining deep.'

Ned pushed his way in, grinning. 'Hey, hey, Annie, you know you can't be studying all weekend long! Ain't that right, 'Omer? It ain't no good for nobody.'

That's a triple negative, which makes it a positive. Studying *is* good for her. Look, she's content. She's never been like this before. Don't spoil it.

Anne-Marie said, 'Can't you find one of the others to go with?'

Ned said, 'The Californians are all saying it's too cold. Where they're from the ocean's as warm as a tub. But nothing ain't too cold for me. I'm from Maine. When we swim in the lake we have to break the ice before we dive in.'

Anne-Marie said, 'It does not sound promising.'

'No, no, Annie, don't get me wrong. I'm telling you, this place I found, it's a jewel. It's paradise. So beautiful. You just won't believe it till you see it.'

'*I'll* come with you,' said Hamish. Flags were dull. Searching for fossils was dull. Ned was fun. 'I'll do the picnic.'

'Very well,' said Anne-Marie, resigned to going too.

Hamish packed baguettes, some cheeses, grapes. Anne-Marie brought her book on Provençal farming techniques of the fifteenth century. Ned led the way along a route he thought he was the first to discover. It was hard work. Hamish got left behind. He didn't mind. Ned was telling Anne-Marie about his research project. It was on some dead French poet.

Hamish was enjoying himself, scrambling over the rocks. He came slithering down a huge one and just missed stepping on two bodies laid out, side by side. The sun was in his eyes, their skins sleek and brown. He thought they were seals. But they were humans, completely naked. They weren't moving. He thought they were dead. Then the female moved her hand to brush a strand of hair from her eyes.

Hamish hurried, heart thumping, to catch up with the others. Ned's route may have been special but it was hardly an unknown secret. Ned's bay, however, was relatively unpopulated and the sunbathers wore costumes. The water was a milky blue, striated with midnight blue. It shimmered with tiny fish.

'See guys,' said Ned. 'What did I tell you? Paradise!' and he punched the air, stripped down to his trunks and rushed in.

Anne-Marie settled in the shade of a pine-tree with her book. Hamish wanted to go in so Ned wouldn't think he was a wimp. But he was scared of what the water might do to him. He was not a strong swimmer.

He went behind a rock to undress. His body had always been a disappointment. Legs: pale, thin, knock-kneed. Chest: concave, skeletal. A louse at Jebb's used to call him Birdcage Boy, because of the ribcage. He scuttled fast for the water so it would cover him. The temperature shocked him, not for the cold but the gentle warmth. Ned was right. And the salinity held him secure. Even without moving, he was buoyant.

He saw Ned swim vigorously out of the bay towards the big sea. He saw Anne-Marie serene under her tree.

He lay on his back and stretched out his arms. It was like resting. The sky overhead seemed to revolve. He saw the translucent moon rising in the east. He watched the languid flight of a gull. He saw the flurry of snowy foam as it touched the rocks. He felt inquisitive fish mouths tickle his thighs. He floated, weightless. He became an unborn baby called Henri, an angel-fish, an amoeba, a microscopic ribbon of plankton, a dolphin. He could be anything.

Ned was swimming back in a strong streamlined crawl. He waved, but Ned had passed him and was powering back to shore. Hamish resolved to swim every day so that all his muscles would grow strong and his lungs increase their power.

He stayed so long in the water that he lost any sense of time until Anne-Marie was calling to him and waving a towel. He doggy-paddled in. She handed him the towel. 'Chéri, what happened? You will be so tired. Are you all right?'

He nodded, proud of his magnificent endurance. His skin was scarcely blue. His teeth were hardly chattering at all though by the time he'd dressed, he was ravenous. Ned, leaning against Anne-Marie's tree, had the remains of the picnic spread out around his feet, a handful of grapes, and the crusty end of a baguette.

Greedy Ned was talking in a quiet, earnest way that Hamish didn't care for. He'd thought Ned was going to be his friend, not hers. She didn't need a companion. She had her medieval bishops. He didn't like the way Ned looked at her. He was glad she hadn't taken off her clothes and gone in the water. That might have changed things. He didn't want anything to change about himself and his mother, not now it had got good.

But nothing stays the same for ever. Change was approaching fast. The big sky still seemed like a bowl of pure light. But had Hamish owned binoculars, he would have seen on the horizon a cluster of grey clouds. Had he understood weather patterns he might have known how, within an hour, an innocent cluster of fluff can gather to a storm.

Gale Force Ten

The wind freshened from a light breeze to a strong breeze which swirled the air, blew away the mist, lifted the water. The boy watched the waves build, till each was higher than a tree, higher than a house, higher than a factory, higher than the tallest building imaginable. Monsieur Bruno had told them how skyscrapers could be so tall that their rooftops were permanently wreathed in cloud but that such buildings were not safe places to be as they were more vulnerable to attack. Nor was sea-level safe. The boy longed to reverse time, to be back in the calm of Monsieur Bruno's class.

No man could smoke a cigarette to calm his nerves. Full concentration, full stamina was required to hold on and remain with the boat. Some began to pray though any sound was whipped from their mouths.

The wind-speed increased to gale force ten. The crest of each wave towered over them, seemed to pause in midair, before crashing down. The wind was so powerful they could scarcely keep their eyes open. The boy made himself keep looking at the violent turmoil. It wasn't a nightmare. It was reality. He had to hold on to it.

The skipper had never experienced such conditions. He was going to lose his boat. He was going to lose his business. He was going to lose his life. He was certain they were all going to die. In this he was wrong. One of them, who'd already lost his nationality, his identity and everything familiar to him which made life worth living, found an inexplicable tenacity for survival.

LANDFALL

Wind in the Rigging

Coppery lightning crackled along the horizon. Thunder rumbled like a faraway herd of running wildebeests. The metal rigging of the pleasure boats began a high-pitched tinkle. At first, the wind only ruffled the water. But soon it was beating it into a foaming soup. The herd was pounding nearer. The sky was blotted out in a dark frenzy, lit by sudden flashes.

He hadn't realized there could be so many categories of lightning. The flat white sheets, the sparkly decorations, the zigzags that dived like cormorants. Then an astonishing crack so close it shook the utensils in the kitchen and knocked out the lights.

He wasn't supposed to hang out in the library. But this was an uncommon situation. He wasn't alarmed for himself but Anne-Marie might need reassurance. You never knew what was going to upset her. If sun and blue sky put her into such ecstasy, heavy weather might be a serious downer.

He found all the Scholars gathering at the open library windows, watching the sea drama while they waited for the electricity to be restored. Another bolt of lightning hit the waves and there were gasps.

'Wowee!'

'Ain't never seen nothing like that before!'

'Don't suppose the Frenchies have either.'

Ned was the expert on weather conditions. 'Hey no!' he contradicted everybody. 'Round here, these storms are commonplace.' And he held forth on the definitions and classifications of storms, gales, hurricanes, cyclones, tornados, then moved on to great storms of history. 'And y'all remember what happened to Saint Paul? And to Ulysses?'

Anne-Marie said with a smile, 'Sose sirens?'

She didn't usually join in their banter.

Ned said sternly, 'I was referring to the shipwreck.'

There were cheers when power was restored. The Scholars returned to their computers.

'No guys! Don't go there!' said Ned. 'You switch off and fast. Gotta protect your hard-drive. If there's another strike your whole caboodle'll blow.'

The power supply didn't last. They were back in the near dark with the intermittent lightning and the sweep of the lighthouse beam. The wind went on picking up speed. The windows flapped. There was a shattering of glass. So they secured the shutters against further breakages. It was too dark to read. The charged atmosphere made it difficult to concentrate. They discussed, debated, argued. Their talk shifted from *Frankenstein* and literary storms to comparative research methodology. Then one of them proposed sharing a pot-luck meal up in her apartment. That was okay by Hamish, so long as he didn't have to join in. He kissed Anne-Marie goodnight. She'd be safe with them. They were reliable mother-sitters so long as she stayed with the whole group and wasn't on her own with just one of them. Specially not with Ned. Ned was going to be *his* special pal, not hers.

He ran across the gardens. The wind whipped at the palm fronds. The rain began to come down in rods, in bucket-loads, in a continuous cascade. It turned the ground into a torrent of gravel, twigs, mud gushing down to the sea.

By the time he got into Les Mimosas, he was drenched. And exhilarated. The howling, booming, thrashing, lashing, crashing outside was tremendous. In bed, he had his Maglite and his Royal National Lifeboat Institution International Code guide-book which he already knew back to front, upside down, from one to ten and from A to Z. Should the need arise, he would be able to communicate with the commander of any vessel without a language barrier. So it was time to proceed to the new hobby. He'd given up on the fossils. Hadn't found a single one. What about pebbles in funny shapes, with holes in the middle? Plenty to sort through on the beach.

He fell asleep unaware that the focus for his new collection was already heading towards him, clinging for life to a piece of timber, and would be reaching land first thing in the morning.

The Undrowned Boy

He had felt the cold before. Of course. Plenty of times. When the dusty dry harmattan from the Sahara blew, making it too hot by day and too cold by night. When he took the fever and shook for three days and nights. When the rains came and stayed too long. When there was no dry fuel left and his mother had to cook the chorba soup over a sulky paraffin flame.

But this European water-chill was of a different category.

Monsieur Bruno had instructed them on many things. He had explained about the world beyond their own villages. The boy understood about other climates. He had never seen snow, and had seen ice only inside the insulated wooden box on the back of the ice-man's bicycle. But he had imagined how it must be in those wide spaces where the Inuit lived, where for more than half the year, there was no earth to be seen, only ice. No water. No lakes or rivers. Where the roads were made of ice. Where the snow heaped up around the people's huts like the grit in a wind-storm. But unlike the smooth glassiness of sand, their snow didn't shift and disperse. Each particle clung to its neighbour and stayed solid as rock all winter. The Inuit people possessed metabolic and circulatory adaptations for their climate. They also had warm sealskin clothes, sealskin boots, oil stoves inside their huts. They had snow dogs that they could embrace to share their body heat.

This numbing cold was lodged solid in the core of his body. It had seeped into his bone marrow, his lungs, his kidneys. It was in the lobes of the brain which Monsieur Bruno had revealed to them on the chart hanging from the nail on the beam at the end of the classroom. In his ears, his eyes, his nostrils, in the joints of his feet, which Monsieur Bruno had not had time to show them.

As soon as he had hit the water, his body had been shocked by the chill. But with so much going on, so much shouting, crying, such terror, he hadn't noticed it then. He had been wearing the uncle's cumbersome jacket over his vest and tee-shirt. And so, despite the extreme cold, he did not succumb to hypothermia. The three layers of garments, although instantly saturated, had acted as insulators, retaining enough body heat.

Another factor contributing to the boy's survival was the salinity of the water. If inhaled, saltwater causes greater lung damage than freshwater. However, it offers greater buoyancy. The Mediterranean has higher salinity than the Atlantic, the Pacific, the English Channel, the Irish Sea, or the North Sea.

He struggled against the waves that were smashing down on him. He must soon die. The sacred words of the Shadada that must be uttered before death came to him. 'la ilah illa Allah wa Muhammad rasul Allah.'

Then, unexpectedly, the clouds parted. For a few moments the moon was illuminating the chaos, revealing the towering height of the waves, the breaking boat, the disappearing head of the last man to drown, and a piece of floating timber. He made a grab. He missed. His head went under. But his limbs went on flailing involuntarily. His face bobbed up. The plank rushed at him on a surge of water. He made a second grab and got a hold.

From Monsieur Bruno he knew that wood is filled with tiny air pockets. This length of plank was a permit to survival. So long as he could keep on to it. He must not loosen his grip. And he must not succumb to sleep.

The storm clouds swirled and covered the moon. The world returned to darkness. He held tight to his wood. He kept his eyes open for the break in the ouds. A sighting of the moon told him he was not alone. This same moon was casting light on his mother. This same moon governed the times of the festivals.

His life-saver nudged against rock. His feet dragged on pebbles. He could not unclasp his arms from around the plank. He must move. When he tried to stand, the touch of the ground on his bare soles was so painful. With hypothermia, even in its milder form, comes drowsiness, irrational behaviour, poor coordination. The blood vessels to the skin contract so that the skin feels cold and hard as stone. He began to crawl up the shingle. He made slow progress and the movement made him nauseous. All the time he was in the boat rocking and swaying, he'd wanted to reach solid land. But here the ground was shifting and swaying under him. He'd been seasick. Now he was landsick.

Higher up the bay, he saw a flat rock which was changing colour from dull grey to pale pink. The sun was rising over the cliffs and targeting the rock. The sun was heating the rock. He had to have that heat. He staggered like a child whose legs are bowed with rickets.

He reached the flat rock. He fell on it and embraced ... an Inuit child holding his dog.

Hamish, Yves and Negative Pastimes

He did not, after all, go sailing with Yves.

'Sorry Oatmeal. Papa has to take the yacht over to the boatyard for its refit.'

'Refit?' What did that mean? How long did it take?

Yves didn't challenge Hamish to a tennis match either. 'I forgot to explain. The club is strictly members only.'

'I better join,' said Hamish.

'You cannot do that. There is a waiting list. Names of under-eighteens have to be put forward to the committee by a responsible adult.'

'I could get Dr Whyte to nominate me.' Hamish knew that the director was exasperated by the presence of a child at the Institut. He was forever reprimanding Hamish for misdeeds that Hamish had not done. When he couldn't think of anything to criticize Hamish for, he'd say, 'Have you nothing better to do than slouch around outside? It's distracting for the scholars.'

Yves said, 'No. He's American. It has to be someone from round here, a member of the local community, not an outsider.'

'Would your father do it for me?'

'Doubt it. You have to be permanent here too. You're only temporary, aren't you?'

'Not necessarily. We *might* stay forever. I know, couldn't I come up to your place and we could have a friendly knockabout on your driveway?'

'No, it's being resurfaced. Listen, if I were you I wouldn't bother with the tennis. It's tedious. I only do it because Papa wants me to. But I'm giving it up.'

The Sun Worshippers

The morning warmed the rock. The rock warmed the boy. He peeled off his two jackets, his two sweaters, and spread them to dry. A man and a woman came along the coast. They took off their sandals and waded through the water to reach their objective. A flat rock in the sun.

They carried a basket and a backpack. They selected their rock. They took off all their garments, then the woman lay face down on the rock. The man lay face up. They were very still. They did not speak. The boy watched. Were they performing a devotional act?

The boy remained with his rock. The couple remained unmoving until the woman suddenly sat up, looked at her wristwatch and began rapidly to unpack the basket. Packets, cartons, plastic containers came out. The colourful foods and bottles of drink were set out round them both. Their rock was not wide. Several items toppled over the edge and had to be rescued.

They ate, looking out to sea, handing each other small pieces of food and laughing. A seagull landed near them. It stood watching closely.

The boy watched too. Now that he was less cold, he thought about hunger. He had eaten bread and dates on the boat. When was that? He had no idea of time. He had to keep watching the couple feasting. He couldn't keep his eyes off them.

His mother could cook pastille, tagine, harira, chakchouka with the eggs, kefta. He could see her pounding coriander and cumin for the harissa. On special occasions they had lamb mechoui, ragout of rabbit.

His clothes dried stiff from the salt. The couple were not watching. They had their backs to him. He pulled on his clothes. His feet and hands were bare and cold. The sun moved round, casting half the bay in shade. The couple picked up their luggage and turned to see if the big flat rock was still occupied. They looked intently at the boy. They spoke to one another, loudly, in a language he didn't know. It wasn't French. It wasn't Arabic. It wasn't Berber, or any of the languages he had heard in the crossings town. Perhaps it was German, or Dutch, or Danish, or another of the languages of the lands of plenty. He didn't take in the meaning of the glaring look till later. If only he had appreciated in good time that they wanted his flat wide rock in full sun more than they wanted their own smaller, sloping rock in the shade, he might have done a deal.

My rock for your jackets, bathing towels, sandals, identity cards or your travel permits? You wouldn't have to speak. It could be done with gestures. But his brain was lethargic. It failed to tell him till too late what could be done.

The couple were putting on their clothes. They were gathering up their towels, hats. It was time for them to move on. The boy watched them hesitate, pointing and deliberating whether to return the way they'd come, or try a more direct route, up the steep rocks, over a wall, and across some gardens. They chose the longer way, down to the water, back along the coast. Their choice was to the boy's advantage. As they scrambled over the rocks, several items bounced out of their basket. He waited till they were out of sight before he went to see what they had dropped.

He feasted ravenously on strangely-soft white bread filled with strange pink meat. Was it pork? The cold had numbed his sense of smell. He peeled the meat off the bread and threw it for the seagull. He ate their tomatoes, their triangle of cheese, their untouched bag of nuts, the over-ripe bananas. There was chocolate. He broke off a square but it made him nauseous.

They had left their newspaper behind. He looked at the pictures. He saw a football team lined up, arms folded, pleased with themselves. They had won their match. Another photo showed men in suits, white shirts, ties, smiling as they shook hands. He supposed they were businessmen who had done a deal that pleased them. Both sides happy. Better than football when only half the players from the field could conclude their day gazing triumphantly at the camera.

He saw a blurry picture of a smashed boat. A uniformed figure was standing by. Was he the owner? Or militia? What was the use of standing guard over half a broken boat? What was the use of looking at that picture?

He returned to his rock. He found a narrow crevice below it, wide enough for his body if he folded his legs. It would not protect him from rain. But it would shield him from wind and from being seen. It was above sea-level. He scrumpled the sheets of newspaper to make a bed-mat. He was cold but he was not wet. Soon he would begin to forget who he was and why he was here.

Post Traumatic Stress Disorder occurs after an individual has been through an event that has caused him extreme anxiety, often accompanied by feelings of horror and a sense of helplessness. Over the past few weeks, the boy had experienced horror, loss, shock, culminating in the overwhelming sense of his own mortal helplessness. He had survived the sea. He had no idea how. He had never heard of Post Traumatic Stress Disorder. Yet he knew he was still terribly at risk. He must take care of himself. Because if he didn't, who else would? He tugged a sheet of newspaper over his head to block out the sight of the water. He must rest. And when he had rested he must go in search of help.

Henri Porridge

The Franco-Scot, too, felt he had endured a prolonged period of stress, of shock and anxiety. He had heard them talk about Post Traumatic Stress Disorder at the clinic when he had to endure that bereavement counselling. He knew that PTSD could be serious, could cause more long-term damage than, say, a smashed leg. However, he also knew that he hadn't had it back then, and he hadn't got it now despite having been through some distressing experiences. The shocking raid on Mr Joel's shop. The unexpected end of Douglas. The constant bullying and thieving at Jebb's. Seeing that camp in the north with those sad asylum kids, that had been a definite jolt to the system. The memory of them, too blank even to kick a ball, still came back at him sometimes. And then those horrible violent riots, even though he'd only seen them on the TV, had definitely affected him.

But he hadn't been overwhelmed to the point of

incapacity. The after-effects had not weakened or permanently damaged him. Perhaps he'd even been strengthened. That's what bad events were supposed to do to you, provided you were tough enough to start with. According to Douglas, anyhow. The resilience of the Scots was a good example. Every time they'd been attacked by the irritating English, they'd boshed them back across the border more strongly.

So if he had, in some way, been improved by his distressing experiences, where was his new determination and inner strength going to take him?

No Particular Pebbles

He went down to start his new collection. It was early. He saw a boy squatting on the big flat rock. He felt mild irritation. The beach should have been deserted. At this time of day, this was always *his* beach. The nudist sunbathers had their special place further on. Hardy hikers like Ned had the pine-tree bay. Keen swimmers went to the deep bay beyond the harbour. Tourists had the main public beach. Men with fishing rods used the outcrop, below the hermit's chapel, where luxuriant seaweed growth provided rich feeding grounds. And this beach, secluded and inaccessible, was for use by people from the Institute. That was what Dr Whyte had told them. It wasn't private but it managed to be exclusive. The bay was too shallow for yachts. And since it couldn't be reached by road, not many visitors knew about it.

The intruder was barefoot. He'd have got quite wet wading through the pools between the rocks. He was staring out to sea, like he was in a trance. Hamish glared. The boy took no notice. So Hamish turned his back and concentrated on the pebble hunt. There were far too many to choose from. They came in three colours. Brownish. Greyish. Whitish. Yet in form, they were all exactly the same. Oval and smooth with no idiosyncrasies. It was beginning to feel like the most futile project he'd ever started. He kicked at the shingle hoping it would make him feel better.

Welcome Committee

The sky was still dark but the surface of the sea was metallic grey, as flat as if rolled from sheets of pressed steel. Today he must find the reception centre. It would have the sign outside, showing the red crescent on the white background, or else the red cross on white. But what if it had some quite other emblem that his father and his uncle hadn't told him about, how would he recognize it?

They shouldn't have treated him like a child. They should have involved him, shared information. His mother had told him to respect his father, that he had been a hero. But if a man's protest fails, if he's wounded in a gun-battle and ends up tipped into the sea, what kind of heroism is that? What is the use of his efforts if there is no one left to celebrate them except a hungry boy, perched upon a rock in a land of plenty?

He found the village. In the soft grey light before dawn, he saw cats sitting on lobster pots and a solitary old man on a bollard who nodded in the boy's direction. Neither hostile nor friendly, but neutral.

He had understood that everything here would be bigger. Yet this harbour was small; just half a dozen fishing boats moored on the jetty. He saw tubs of flowers. He saw no police, no militia, no customs house, nobody resembling law-enforcement personnel.

He saw a sign on a glass door. 'Réception', it said. His heart gave a small jolt of hope. Had he found it? He ran over and tried the door. It was locked. He pressed his nose to the glass. The hallway was dusty and unlit. Mail and colourful advertisements lay on the tiled floor. *Hôtel les Falaises* was stamped in black on the doormat. A pencilled card was stuck inside the door. *Fermeture Annuelle. Ouverture: Pâques*. It was a hotel, closed till the new season.

His feet were white with cold. He was disheartened. He passed a bakery. It too was closed. But he could smell bread and in the interior beyond the shop-front, he saw a man in white, kneading dough. Didn't bakers sometimes have unsold leftovers from the previous day? He tapped on the glass. The baker couldn't hear. He knocked harder. The baker went on kneading and shaping his loaves, engrossed in his work. The smell of bread was almost unbearable.

The boy continued down the narrow street, saw a sleepy old woman opening the shutters on an upper floor, but found nothing that resembled a red crescent or a red cross.

He left the main street behind and came to a two-storey building with a courtyard. The gate was open. In the courtyard, a caretaker in a blue overall was sweeping leaves, just as the boy and his classmates used to do to help Monsieur Bruno. Back there, Monsieur Bruno was caretaker as well as teacher. This was a nursery for very small children. There were coloured activity toys in the courtyard, animal shapes stuck in the windows. But no little children, no teachers. The boy crossed the courtyard. He spoke slowly and clearly to the man.

'Bonjour, monsieur. Can you please direct me to the nearest reception centre for new arrivals?'

The man turned, as if surprised to see somebody behind him, nodded, then resumed his sweeping. The boy repeated his question. The caretaker waved his arm in a confusing circular gesture and made a strange noise in his throat. It wasn't speech. The fellow was a mute. There'd never be a comprehensible answer out him until you grew familiar with his signs.

'Merci, monsieur. Merci.'

e tried not to let despair overwhelm him. He had

no idea what to do. He made his way painfully back to his point of arrival. If he could only have understood the mute's gestures, and if only he had had the strength to walk four kilometres beyond the village, he would have reached the quarry. He might have recognized the makeshift shantytown as his true home from home.

He crouched in his angle between the rocks. It was the nearest he had to a home. It was the time for Soobh Fegr. 'Praise be to God, Lord of the world, the compassionate, the merciful, King of the day of judgement.' He couldn't remember what came next. Soon he would begin to forget why he was here.

Post Traumatic Stress Disorder brings with it the relief of forgetfulness. This amnesia may be selective when the victim eradicates only those events which are most unbearable. Or it may become random and spasmodic. There will be reduced interest in everyday events, poor concentration, an increased reaction to small frights, insomnia even when the person is suffering extreme fatigue. There will be irritability, mounting to inexplicable bouts of anger which can turn to lassitude. What a mix-up.

The boy crouched with his arms around his knees. He rocked back and forth, imitating the movement of the waves which might lull him into peace. He did not know who he was. Once, he had been advised to forget his name and take a new one. He was forgetting all his names. Everything familiar was going away. And there was nothing to take its place.

Beach Clearances

A succession of storms made a mess of the famously lovely coast. The bodies didn't come ashore conveniently, together in a group, but washed in on different days, in varying conditions, at widely dispersed arrival positions. Each time another one turned up, the area was flashing with blue lights, screaming with sirens, buzzing with officers. If it was at a point inaccessible by road, the air and the sea became busy with the whirring of helicopter blades and the swish of speeding rescue launches.

Hamish didn't see any of the victims. But he heard about them. Ned discovered one on a coastal hike. Hamish asked about it. He was curious because he hadn't been allowed to see Douglas's body.

Ned said, 'Poor guy didn't look so pretty. The law took their time arriving but once they were there they got him zipped into his body-bag pdq. Seems like the officials ignore these inky guys so long as they keep themselves to themselves. They're cheap labour. But once they're dead mutton, they get plenty attention.'

Curious fish swept north from warmer waters were a matter for the Fish Tribunal. Human floaters were the concern of the police. Even though it is well known that when dead men come out of the sea it's because they've drowned, investigation was required in order to demonstrate that no villainy, violence or foul play was involved.

The other storm rubbish was a municipal matter.

The main bathing beach was cleansed each morning. Normal procedure was to gather up picnic rubbish off the shingle, empty the refuse-bins, replace the plastic liners, rake the sand, spray-clean the promenade steps. More flotsam than usual was coming ashore. Torn tee-shirts, fir-cones, lengths of twisted twine, an armless doll, drink cans, broken espadrilles, lolly sticks, dead fish, bathing-shoes, tattered beach mats, fluorescent-yellow fishing nets, driftwood, everything gift-wrapped in raggedy green strips of the Neptune grass.

On smaller bays, the municipal workers' tidy-up was perfunctory. They checked there was nothing valuable in the drift of debris, changed bin-liners, moved on.

Hamish and the Boy

The boy who'd appropriated the bay was no longer barefoot but wearing designer trainers with the zazzy fluorescent logo on the side.

'Salut!' Hamish called.

The boy didn't reply.

'New shoes. Sensationelle! D'you get them in the village? Didn't know they sold such mondo clobber.'

The boy still said nothing, and was deliberately avoiding eye-contact.

'Or did you nick them? Come on, I won't snitch on you.' Then Hamish noticed that the trainers were different sizes, one with a flappy sole, the other almost new, and he was annoyed by his own slowness. He should've realized. The boy had sifted through beach-debris to find them.

Hamish noticed a trickle of blood on the boy's forehead, a gash, just above the hairline. 'Did you know

211

you've got a cut on your head? You ought to get it seen to.'

The boy didn't seem bothered by the wound. Perhaps it didn't hurt.

Hamish said, 'You do understand French, don't you?'

The boy's eyes flickered. He had obviously understood.

'Thought so. Well, you know that this beach is private, don't you? See the sign? Propriété Privée. Reserved for the use of residents who have access from their residencies. Are you staying in one of the villas up there? No, don't suppose you are. You're not local, are you?'

The boy got up and moved further away. This was even more irritating than not replying. Worse than irritating. It was downright rude. Hamish followed him.

'And you're not at the Collège Mistral. I'd recognize you if you were. And you'd know me. I'm the only British pupil there.'

'Not from here,' said the boy. He looked down at his feet in the ridiculous mismatched trainers.

'Where you from then?'

The boy suddenly became agitated. 'No more questions. No, no, no!' he said and scrambled away over the rocks, with the too-large trainer slip-slopping on one foot as it tried to keep in step with the trainer on the other foot.

Hamish scooped up a fistful of pebbles that weren't worth the bother of becoming collectors' items and he started to skim them, one by one, just past the boy's shoulder towards the sea. He wanted to create a bit of a splash. But after he'd watched the fan of spray spurt up out of the flat surface and spatter down again a dozen times and the boy still didn't react, he wished he hadn't bothered. It was just a waste of his effort, the sort of feeble wind-up boys used to do to him at Jebb's. They'd pitch their sharpened pencils across the classroom at him, just to startle him, to make him think they were going to hit him. Occasionally he'd done the same to Watkins. There was always a pecking order, like with chickens in their overcrowded hut.

So who was at the bottom of the pecking order? There always had to be someone right underneath, who had no one else to pick on, a passive person who never fought back.

Yves, Pierre
and Luc

Hamish went down to fetch the evening baguette. He bumped into Yves with two other guys, coming out of the boulangerie as Hamish was about to go in.

'Salut, Porridge,' said Yves.

Hamish couldn't ignore him. The doorway was too narrow, and the soft-centred boulanger's wife was watching them from behind her glass-fronted chill-cabinet displaying almond pastries, éclairs, mille-feuilles, chocolate nègres en chemises.

'Salut, Froggy,' he said, hoping the offence would register.

Yves said, 'Hé, Oatmeal, you like the blacks?'

'The blacks?' What was Yves on about? Had he found out about what had happened to Douglas? Or about Anne-Marie's abduction in her car? Hamish did not want Yves knowing things about his past that he hadn't told him.

He said, stiffy, 'I don't have an opinion on the matter.'

'You should,' said Yves. 'But then one expects porridge to be invertebrate.' Then he went swaggering off down the street with Pierre and Luc, as if they owned the place.

Hamish must not allow himself to be so easily affronted. Sticks and stones, and all that.

'Bonsoir, madame,' he said to the baker's wife.

'Bonsoir, jeune homme,' she replied.

'And how are you today, madame? Yes, one baguette, s'il vous plaît.'

'Voilà, monsieur.'

'Merci, madame.'

Why, what a pleasant, polite young man he knew he was. Quite unlike the uncouth froggies.

Yves and the Poetry

Lunch at the Collège Mistral was a gastronomical feast. On the dot of midday, three full courses and as much baguette from the bread-basket as you could eat. But then came the drag, récré. Two hours' long. You had to stay out in the courtyard the whole time. They locked the main doors of the building to make sure.

Hamish couldn't take the afternoon heat. While other boys dashed around playing football like hot mad dogs, he squatted on his haunches in the shade and tried to go through the poem they'd been set. You weren't allowed to bring your workbooks into the cour de récréation so the words had to be held inside your head.

The poem was about a fisherman's love for the sea which gave him his livelihood. It was by some great Frenchman. Hamish could see a small distant stripe of sea. He'd noticed how it never remained the same, not from one hour to the next, let alone one minute to another. Its colours varied according to sky-colour. The surface patterns changed, the nearness and farness of the horizon, the ways in which boats moved through the waves. But he'd not considered how you might describe these differences, the words you could use. And now, here they were, twelve verses long, a different sea-mood in every stanza. The variety of vocabulary made the learning-by-heart a challenging task.

Yves sauntered across the cour de récré. He stood in front of Hamish providing additional and welcome shade. He clicked his knuckles but without having anything to say.

'Salut, Frogleg,' said Hamish eventually.

'Salut, Oatmeal,' said Yves.

'You okay?' Hamish asked.

'Oui. Ça va.'

'Good,' said Hamish.

'And you okay too?'

'Oui, merci,' said Hamish, and he thought, We have absolutely nothing in common, you and I. You have your loathing of study, your contempt for tennis. I have fewer advantages than you so I have less to loathe.

Yves said, 'Porridge, what are you doing squatting down there like an Indian guru?'

'Seeing to that poem Monsieur Ponchaud set us.'

Yves was incredulous. 'You're not memorizing it!'

'That is what he asked us to do. It is not hard.' Hamish recited the first stanza.

Yves gawped as if he'd seen a conjuring trick. 'How did you do that?'

'I read it through. Then say it over enough times till it sticks. Takes a bit of time, say, a couple of hours.'

Yves said, 'I don't have that kind of free time. I'm always busy with stuff when I'm home. Anyway, it's easy enough for you. You're a foreigner. You've had to practise learning to pick up our language. You're experienced at receiving new words. I bet Monsieur Ponchaud will make one of *us* be the clown who has to stand for the recitation. He should make you but he won't, will he? He never does. D'you pay him to leave you alone? You better sit behind me after récré. Change places with Guillaume. Then if Ponchaud picks me you can help me out. D'accord?'

'D'accord.'

The conversation was over but Yves went on standing there making the dry noise with his knuckle-bones. He had something else on his mind. The group he'd been with were looking expectantly towards him. Eventually Yves came out with it.

'Hé, Invertebrate Porridge Soup, do you like the blacks?'

'You asked me that yesterday.'

'And today I am checking your consistency.'

'I told you,' said Hamish. 'I have no opinion.' But he felt angry and couldn't staunch it. He shouted at Yves, 'Okay, I do have an opinion. I hate the blacks. A black woman killed my father. A black boy stole my pen that was worth a lot of money. Two black boys took my mother hostage. I hate them all.'

Yves said in a steady tone, 'You are wrong, very wrong.'

'It's true. All that stuff really happened.'

'Okay. I believe you. And it was unfortunate for you. But the Blacks are okay. At least you can trust the Blacks. They're cool. Specially the Americans.' He rattled off the names of some US sportsmen, some US film actors, and a couple of jazz singers. 'Listen, Porridge, it is the Arabs you got to watch out for.'

'The Arabs?'

'He is an Arab, your little pal.'

Hamish thought, How was I to know? He said, 'I don't know what you're talking about.'

'Sure you do. We have all seen you, hanging around that guy. Keep away from him if you know what's good for you. Don't say I haven't warned you.'

Hamish felt his fury boiling up like lava. What right did Yves have to come telling him what he mustn't do?

Hamish was an honorary American. Everybody knows that Americans rule the world.

Yves returned to his sniggering group. Hamish returned to the fifth stanza where the full moon of the autumn equinox rises, glowing red as Mars, to illuminate the lone fisherman. The stanza was richly packed with the category of vocab that Hamish was unlikely to find a use for. Shimmering, ululating, quivering, pulsating, glowing, phosphorescent, lustrous, glossy.

Hamish and the Canapés

Anne-Marie was animated. She had received, from Dr Whyte, a gilt-edged invitation card. Hamish's name, in thick black ink, was at the top next to hers.

'Chéri, my love, look! A soirée, with cocktails and musical entertainment.'

Hamish knew what a soirée was. But what exactly was a cocktail?

'It is a type of drink. Several alcoholic drinks stirred together.'

Hamish did not think it sounded like a heap of fun. 'Not exactly Whipsnade,' he said glumly.

Anne-Marie said, 'But see, he's inviting *you* too!'

'I don't drink alcohol mixtures, as you know.'

'Please come too. He wants you there. Or he wouldn't have invited you. Give it a try and if it's boring you can come back here.'

The Scholars each received their invitation. They discussed the forthcoming event enthusiastically. They discovered from the director's personal assistant that the purpose of the gathering was for clever young minds of the future to meet and mingle with significant local dignitaries, and vice versa.

'So you will come, won't you, sweetheart?'

He said, 'Very well, since I have no other engagements that evening.'

She giggled and kissed him.

Later, she ironed his shirt and her sunflower skirt and she tucked a red hibiscus blossom in her hair.

'You look nice, Maman,' he said because it was so good when she was happy.

'Merci, chéri. Tu es très gentil.'

He liked to hear her say that he was kind even when he knew it wasn't true.

For her sake, he struggled into the crisp white shirt that smelled of hot cotton, and he allowed her to arrange his hair. 'It is an honour that Dr Whyte has included you. There are going to be some important public figures there. The mayor is among the guests.'

'And his son?'

'I should not think so. You are special to have been invited.'

The Scholars dressed up as stylishly as they could manage, given that they had arrived with their cases packed with books rather than finery. But silk scarves were twisted into camisole tops, ties neatly knotted, shoes polished, chins shaved and splashed with cologne. Lipsticks and clothes, blushers and curlers were shared about. Hamish persevered with stanzas nine and ten of the long poem about the robust fisherman, trying to ignore female scholars who dashed in and out of Les Mimosas to borrow or to lend.

On Saturday evening they gathered outside the Grande Salle so as to enter in a safe group. They seemed nervous of mingling with local citizens. Hamish realized that he was the only one who got to meet the natives every school day.

'Hi, hi!' said Ned. 'And don't we all look just so fine and dandy!' He smelled of musk and nutmeg. Hamish feared the power of the aftershave might trigger a breathing attack.

'Hi, hi! Swellegant, elegant!'

'Ain't we just the tops!'

A procession of chauffeur-driven cars was proceeding at walking-pace through the main gates and up to the Institut entrance.

No way could the Scholars have competed in allure with the dignitaries. They stepped from their limousines like exotic birds, dressed in silks and velvets, embroidered moiré and spangled satin. Their necks and ears and wrists jangled with gold and silver decorations, sparkled with diamonds and emeralds, were shiny with splendid medals.

Inside the Grande Salle it was equally glittery, dazzly, shimmery. The crystal chandeliers sparkled. A quartet of merry musicians played on the dais. A team of waiters, impassive-faced, starched jackets, slicked-back hair, served champagne cocktails from behind a mirrored bar.

Dr Whyte, in a shiny plum tuxedo and floral bow-tie, received guests at the top of the stairway. He beamed around like a satisfied lighthouse, greeting Anne-Marie with a kissy action to each cheek, pumping Ned's arm, tousling Hamish's hair.

'Great to have you join us, Sunshine,' he said. 'It's going to be a night to remember, something you'll look back on with amazement when you're an old fellow like me!'

'Oui, monsieur. Merci, monsieur.' Dr Whyte addressed Hamish in English. Hamish liked to reply in French.

'So how's about, young fellow—' Dr Whyte paused to kiss another female guest. 'So how's about you go help yourself to something tasty, then lend a hand with the canapés?'

'Oui, monsieur. D'accord.'

So where were the usual crabby reprimands? What was all this exaggerated avuncular affection? Hamish crushed a handful of olives into his mouth, then asked one of the waiters for instruction. The aloof manners were an affectation. The waiter gave Hamish a surreptitious wink. Hamish recognized him. Fisherman at dawn. Hired servant at dusk. He pointed Hamish towards a dish artfully arranged with miniature savouries. Shrimps perched in the flaky-pastry castles. Sardines were impaled on sticks. Black fish-eggs glistened on toast triangles.

The silver dish was cumbersome, a two-hander job. Hamish set out on his errand of distribution.

'It's got to stop!' a woman in a green sparkly dress screeched in his ear.

'Indeed so, madame,' agreed a man near her. 'Out of control.'

'And who pays for them? That's what I'd like to know.'

Hamish was accustomed to listening in on the Scholars' conversations. When they talked with such intensity about syntaxiquentially emblemated narratives, decontextualizations, psychonarrativality, and pictorial intertextualities, they would from time to time cast him a chummy smile, like a chewy biscuit to a puppy, to let him know that he was not excluded.

Here was different. Not just excluded but invisible. The beautiful people saw the shiny dish he held out. The sweep of their eyes took in the array of dainty delicacies. They did not see any person behind the dish. They carried on with their talk as if he were not present.

Yachts. Vineyards. Canadian ski conditions. Next season's harvest. Opera in Verona. Opera in Sydney. As Hamish toured the room, proffering the dish of titbits, he picked up snatches of their conversations.

'And is Sydney the new Verona?'

He realized that the combination of white shirt, clean hands, tidy hair, impassive expression, silent mouth, created his complete camouflage.

'Of course something's got to be done!' a woman said, before popping an anchovy sandwich into her mouth and reaching out a claw-hand for another. Her upper torso was nearly as exposed as the sun worshippers on naturists' bay.

Hamish turned his head away. It was embarrassing to have to look at a body like that. Right next to her, similarly décolleté, stood an ancient creature with flesh as yellow as a naked chicken from the market.

'The situation is indeed becoming intolerable,' she croaked.

A man, fully clothed in military uniform, agreed. 'It's

a big problem for all of us. And they have it worse further along the coast.'

Hamish was impressed by the quantity of canapés the people consumed. With so much talk to be got through, they obviously needed to keep up their energy levels. He had to go back and back again to the serving table to fetch fresh supplies. Practice makes perfect. Soon he was gliding through the seething throng as adeptly as a springtime salmon swimming up the Tweed. The waiters, too, were hard at work lubricating the talkers.

'It is my opinion that they have all got to go.' It was the mayor wearing his tricolor sash of responsibility, speaking, Yves's father, who had tried to make Hamish not see the huts in the quarry. Now it was Hamish himself, who was indistinguishable from any other serving person.

'We must take a tough line.'

'We cannot be seen to collude.'

Hamish paused to check on Anne-Marie. She was keeping near the tall windows which opened on to the terrace. She was in conversation with two Scholars, and with the photographer who'd been taking pictures of VIPs. She looked fine. Ned was at some distance, talking to the harbourmaster and two ladies whose dresses were so low at the front that

Hamish couldn't help staring, then had to look away.

He went to fetch another laden platter. This time, small oven-hot items. Écrevisses in batter. Miniature sausages wrapped in ham. Roasted snails inside their shells. The dish was hot too. Hamish was amazed how fast those garlic snails went.

'It's the organized trafficking we must combat. There should be a dedicated patrol along the perimeter of all territorial waters. Other countries do it. Craft should be intercepted in time and kept out of our sight.'

'There should be a proper, designated place to put them. But it's definitely not here. It will kill the tourism. The hoteliers are already complaining. Robert Cheval, manager at the Plage d'Or, says he's losing hand over fist.'

Was it a distortion caused by the high noise-level or were these Froggies all discussing the same topic?

'Not only Cheval. Everybody round here is in the same boat.'

'It is vital for our survival to segregate them from the tourists.'

'People come here to relax. They don't want to be upset seeing these desperate destitutes. I belive they should be assisted. But not here.'

'Has anybody considered the terrorism aspect? They

may claim to be asylum seekers. How can we tell? They all look the same.'

'And what about the disease factor? Aids. Hep B. Tuberculosis. There's been another case of meningitis down at the bidonville.'

Bidonville. What was that? He knew he'd heard the word before.

'They were going to build a reception centre. Thankfully, the protest succeeded.'

'The mayor's been using his own launch for patrols. He's been known to tow craft back out to sea. Off the record of course. But unfortunately, our harbourmaster is not in favour. He says it is his duty to assist any stricken craft that come within sight.'

The next dish was oysters, lying alive inside their pearly shells, nestling upon their bed of crushed ice, decorated with lemons sculpted to look like roses. A cold silver dish can be as hard to handle as a hot one. Oysters on ice slipped down even better than hot snails.

A big man in a navy blazer with gilt buttons but no medals replaced his empty oyster shell on Hamish's plate. 'Throughout Europe,' he said, 'the numbers have doubled, I repeat, doubled, since nineteen seventy-five.' He selected another oyster. 'There are now fifty-six million, that's million, in Europe. Can we take any more?

I rather think not.' He threw back his head, poured the living bi-valve and its liquor down his throat.

One of the Scholars joined the discussion. His French was not fluent. 'But surely,' he started tentatively, 'migration is an essential component of any vigorous economy? Managed migration can benefit both individuals and society?'

The blazer man rounded on him. 'It's all very well for you to speak like that, monsieur, but how would you feel if this was your country and they were crawling all over *your* garden?'

An older woman spoke. 'And who pays for them? *We* do! Increased taxes all the time. *We* are paying for these freeloaders!'

They were becoming heated. Another woman joined in, more calmly. 'They will go on coming whatever we do. There is no stopping them. But if they come *here*, then they must adapt to *our* cultural orientation. They must learn our language, our civil code, accept our values, and doctrines. This idea of creating a multi-cultural European society is total romanticism. It cannot succeed.'

After the oysters, there were chocolate truffles and fruit patisseries to be handed round, and champagne. Then a woman in coloured feathers and black gloves stood on the dais and sang songs about love.

At the end of the evening, as Anne-Marie and Hamish were leaving, Dr Whyte came and patted Hamish on the shoulder.

'Bravo. Excellent work. The lads couldn't have managed without you.'

Several Scholars came back to Les Mimosas. Ned said he'd rustle up corn fritters and beef hash. Hamish wasn't hungry. He left Ned opening cans, the others talking, and he went to bed. He was feeling inexplicably desolate. He couldn't understand it. Why should he be sad? The others had all been saying what a great party it had been.

He peeked through the shutter louvers at the still night. He could see the foamy white of the waves breaking against the rocks and the twinkle of distant cruise-ships. Where were they heading? And was that boy still down there in his crevice in the rocks?

Hamish's Disconsolance
with the Echinoderms

On Sunday Anne-Marie went over to the library, same as every other day. This sameness was becoming oppressive. Hamish observed the same calm sea, the usual cloudless sky, the monotonous dance of boats in the port de plaisance, the gull swooping by with its hungry eye, if not the same as the previous one, then identical to it.

The extraordinary had become ordinary. Everything he saw was jaundiced with familiarity.

He watched the boy. Still there, same as ever, poking around searching for stuff. He resolved to go and check up on him. But by the time he had run down the stairs, across the hallway, through the gardens and out on to the rocks, the boy had disappeared from sight.

Hamish had to search hard before he spotted him, crouching in a gap in the rocks, a larger crevice than he had been in before, but more sheltered. The boy was looking towards him so he raised his hand and waved. The boy gave no acknowledgment of the greeting even though he seemed to have been watching out for him. Hamish scrambled over towards him.

'Salut,' he said. 'So you're still around then?'

He'd made the rock-hole into a sort of lair, lined it with plastic bags and a roof of cardboard. It looked almost cosy.

'Do you sleep here? Is this where you've decided to live?'

The boy shrugged. No reply.

'So what's your name?'

The boy shook his head.

'You're very good at silence. I told you my name the other day. Hamish. Why won't you tell me yours? Or don't you have one?'

Another indifferent shake of the shoulders.

'I suppose you want me to call you No-Name? A boy at collège says you're all called Ali.'

What, in point of fact, Yves had said was that all the Arabs shared the same sly, dirty habits, along with the same name, and that he knew this because his father sometimes had to work with them.

'That cut on your head isn't getting any better. You don't want it to get infected.'

Still nothing. He really was extremely passive.

Perhaps he was quite dim. Or perhaps the bash on the head had knocked out some of his brain-cells.

Hamish said, 'If you can't tell me your name, I suppose I'll have to call you Ali. I've worked out who you are. You are one of those sans-papiers people. I am sure you are. One of the illegals. Because you have no papers to prove who you are, do you? Round here they talk a lot about sans-papiers. Well, listen Ali, you have rights. Everybody has rights.'

To Hamish's astonishment, the boy reacted. 'I have no rights,' he said.

'Of course you do. Everybody does. There's something called the Universal Declaration of Human Rights. It's like a kind of world law. And it means that every person wherever they live has the right to certain basic things. Like life, civil liberties, freedom, security of person, whatever that means. There's thirty clauses. I think it's thirty. I can't remember them all but I've got them printed on a special commemorative United Nations flag.'

'I am not from here. I have no entitlement to these rights.'

Hamish said, 'Yes you do. Young people have rights. Not as many, but we still have some. They passed a special convention on the rights of the child. We've got the right to protection from maltreatment, the right to a decent home, education, enough food, even if it's not exactly our favourite type of meal.'

'This is not the law where I lived.'

'That is a very defeatist attitude, Ali. If the adults where you come from didn't accept the charter concerning young persons' human rights, you should have kicked up a fuss, fought for your rights.'

'No fighting. There was already too much fighting.'

It was the longest exchange they'd had. Almost a conversation. But then he fell silent again with his head down.

Hamish continued speaking French. 'Alors, mon ami Ali. I cannot sit here all day long while you are meditating like a monk. I am a man of action. So I am off to search for sea urchins. I saw a diver further along the other day, with a snorkel. He came up with a whole bagful. And I have seen people eating them in the cafés round the harbour. They seem to enjoy them. But I have no clue what they are like. So you want to come?'

The boy who probably wasn't Ali moved his head imperceptibly. 'To eat?' he said.

'Yes. Why not? We could take them back to my place, or just stay on the beach and eat them straightaway.'

The boy hadn't actually said yes and hadn't said no but when Hamish got to his feet, he got up too.

'It's over this way,' said Hamish and set out along the jagged coastline. The boy followed hard on his heels, almost step for step over each rock. The reticence was a bit irritating, but not half as bad as the alternative, aggression and control, like Yves. It was good to have someone tagging on behind, like a dog following its master.

Hamish said, 'I don't think we get them back home. The sea's too cold. Though we've got loads of other kinds of fish. We'll have to go in the water to collect them. They live on the rocks. They look like spiky chestnuts. I haven't a clue how you open them up. Don't suppose you know? Could be they're like oysters and we need a special type of cutter. I don't know if you have to kill them somehow before you eat them.'

Without Hamish noticing how, the boy had taken the lead so now it was Hamish who was panting along, struggling to keep up. 'Seems like you know your way around pretty well, Ali,' Hamish said, pausing for a breather.

The boy went forging ahead. Why was he so eager to find sea urchins? Hamish's own enthusiasm for marine-echinoderm gathering was rapidly diminishing. The prospect of having to eat them alive and wriggling, if that was indeed what they did, was not attractive. 'Maybe we needn't actually *eat* them?' he called. 'We could just catch some to study?'

They rounded the headland. The pastel houses of the village were way behind, hidden from view. Ahead was increasingly rugged coastline, overhung with twisty pines. It felt thrillingly far from civilization. Hamish imagined they were alone on an uninhabited island, fending for themselves.

'Just round the next bend, that's the cove where I saw the diver with the big catch,' Hamish said. They rounded the headland. The cove, far from being deserted, was heavily populated. Every area of level limestone was carpeted with coloured beach towels and reclining bodies.

They weren't the total naturists, but there were a lot of topless females, nonchalant in their semi-nakedness. This was no place to hang around with a boy you didn't know.

Hamish said, 'We better push on a bit further. Find our own personal space?'

The boy was no keener to linger than Hamish was. He backtracked and darted for the safety of a path worn in the rocks which Hamish hadn't noticed. It led them through the pines, under a barbed-wire fence, across a strip of terraced garden. The boy seemed quite sure of himself. He'd obviously been along here before.

Then their route was barred by a woman pruning a

palm in a pot. When she saw them, she was angry.

'You two!' she yelled. 'Off my property. Now! You're all the same, you lot. Go! Or I call security!'

So much for the right to freedom of movement.

The boy led the way easily back to the Institut gates. It wasn't as far off as Hamish had imagined. There were no desert islands. Civilization was all around them.

Ali in Warm Water

The boy was in no hurry to return to his den in the rocks. He hung around the automatic gate as if waiting to see what Hamish would do next.

'Did you know, you've begun to smell quite strong?'

The boy said nothing.

'Yves, the person I was telling you about before, says all Arabs smell bad because – well I don't know why. He just said it. Is it true?'

The boy said, 'Perhaps it is because I have no toileting facilities in my residence. There is only the sea in which to wash.'

Hamish laughed because it was almost a joke. The boy lives in a crevice in a rock and says he has no facilities.

'So do you want to come up to my apartment, Ali, and take a shower?'

It was unsettling to have been yelled at by that woman and made to feel as surplus to requirements as

Ali was. But now, offering Ali the chance to take a shower made him feel warm and magnanimous. He wondered if Yves was up at his villa, watching from the terrace by his pool. He hoped he was. He needed to be shown that Hamish wasn't going to be told who he could hang out with and who he couldn't.

When Hamish opened the door into Les Mimosas and Ali stepped in, Hamish thought he detected approval.

'Oui, oui, oui. I know it is très agréeable here. We are fortunate. But you have to understand this apartment is only temporary accommodation. We cannot stay here forever.'

'Where will you eat your meal?'

'Out on the balcony usually. There are just the two rooms. And it is not like it is our real chez-nous. It is more like a student lodging. Monsieur le Directeur tolerates me being here because my mother is smart and diligent.'

Hamish noticed Anne-Marie's wallet on her bookshelf. She always left it so he could take what was needed for buying their provisions. While Ali was in the shower-room, Hamish hid the wallet between two books, just in case some of the things Yves said were true. Then he got out his collection of classic film posters.

As he expounded on the provenance of each faded film advert, Ali appeared to be paying attention, but it was disappointing not to manage to raise a single pertinent question from him.

Like at Eglantine Jebb's when he'd done his SPP, Special Project Presentation, those dullards hadn't had a word to say. Did these celebrated posters mean nothing to this foreigner? Hamish rolled them back into their protective cardboard cylinders.

Ali said, 'At what time do you eat your meal?'

He said, 'Not for ages. Not till my mother gets back. Don't you have films, where you come from? I would have thought that even if it is a bit of a backward place, you might at least have old film shows from time to time?'

The boy said, 'I know what cinema is.'

Next, Hamish brought out the flag collection. Ali didn't have a word to say about the flags. He looked at them, but more as if watching ghosts dancing. He asked, 'Where do you sleep? Where does your family sleep?'

Hamish said, 'I told you. There are me and Maman. C'est tout. Nous deux, c'est la famille. And you can not stay here, if that was what you were fishing for. No way. We would be thrown out. She would not finish her dissertation. It would be le grand désastre.'

When Hamish went downstairs to let Ali out through the automatic gates, he took care to keep the number pad hidden under his hand as he tapped in the code because the mayor might have been correct about the thieving nature of Arabs.

A Pestering Beggar

At the end of the day, the bus dropped them off by the big white rock outside the Institut gates, same as usual.

'Salut,' said Yves.

'Salut,' replied Hamish.

'À demain,' said Yves.

'À demain,' echoed Hamish.

Even when the association has cooled, the social niceties persist. Yves started off up the slope towards his villa. He suddenly turned and called out, 'Hé, Porridge. Voilà! There he is again. I warned you he'd be hanging around.'

Hamish looked. The boy was hiding in the narrow space between two wheelie-bins. He was so thin he fitted easily. His eyes were to the ground, as though, if he didn't look out, he could make himself unseen.

'He is on the scrounge,' Yves said.

'I told him I would bring him bread.'

'Bread?'

'From the dinner hall.' Hamish pulled some pieces of stale baguette from his pocket.

'You took that from our collège?'

'The staff throw it out if it's not eaten.'

'It belongs to the state. You stole it. You're as bad as one of them.'

The boy had withdrawn so far back into the small space between the bins that he was no longer visible.

'Okay, you give him the stolen bread,' said Yves angrily. 'See if I care. I shall not snitch. But you should not feed them. Never. That is what my father says. It only encourages them.' Then he ran home.

Hamish went over to the wheelie-bins. Ali reached out for the bread without a word. Hamish thought, Maybe Yves is right. Perhaps he *is* like a dog. A scabby mongrel, sniffing around the bins. The boy's face was beginning to look pinched and mean. Almost ferrety. Or did it only appear that way because Yves had put the idea of Arabs all being like dogs into his mind?

The boy came after Hamish to the gates. 'Do you have anything else? I am very hungry.'

Hamish tapped the entry code onto the numeral pad. The boy was sticking close. Was he going to try and follow Hamish in right now? Or was he trying to make out the digits to remember for later? Or was he, as he claimed, just hungry? Or, as he seemed, desperately alone?

With an electronic click-click, the mechanism unlocked itself. Hamish darted in and closed the gate behind him.

'No, Ali, or whatever your name is.' Hamish spoke through the railing. 'You cannot come in. That time before was an exception. I was breaking the rules. Nobody is allowed in until they have been checked. IDs and all that. This place is an institution. Not an ordinary home.' He thought, And why do you pester me? Why not choose some other person?

The boy remained there, clutching the bars with both hands like he was imprisoned in the outside world. Although he was free to walk away he went on peering through the gate like a ravenous hound.

'Listen Ali, you must find yourself a better place. More agreeable.'

'*What* more agreeable place?'

'There must be somewhere. You cannot stay on the rocks for ever.'

'There is no reception centre here. I have asked. There is no one who can speak to me of my situation. Any person I have tried to speak with, they would rather I did not exist, just went away.'

Hamish said, 'Have you tried the quarry yet? You might find someone there who can advise you. D'accord?'

Ali stared in through the bars with his big brown eyes, sadder than the saddest person on earth. Was it all put on, Hamish wondered, to force him to feel sorry for him? Or could the boy really and truly be quite alone without any family? Surely not. He couldn't be more than twelve or thirteen. That kind of thing didn't happen, except in wars.

'Very well,' Hamish said. 'I'll bring you something down. But you cannot come in here again.' He hurried into the building and up the stairs. He closed the door of Les Mimosas. He warmed some milk in a pan, mixed it up with the powdered cocoa and made a large bowlful of drinking chocolate. He cut a slice of brioche and wrapped it in a piece of foil. But when he went down to the gate with his offering the boy had gone. With any luck, he'd taken himself off to the quarry, just like Hamish had suggested.

Hamish went back up to the apartment and sat on the balcony and ate the cake and drank the warm chocolate drink. He saw some rustling under the trees. It could have been a pair of magpies fighting, though the movement seemed too vigorous for birds. Perhaps it was a cat. He watched two fishing boats chugging out of the harbour, one behind the other. He watched two sailing boats gliding into harbour.

I hate it here. Really hate it. I don't belong. I want to be somewhere else. I want to go home. I'm trapped in this French life when I'm really Scottish. *I'm* the one who's imprisoned.

WONDERLAND

Ali and Ali in
the Quarry

Each hut was home to five or six men. Not one resident was willing to engage with him. Then he spotted a boy emerging from one of the smallest huts and approached him. The other boy was taller than himself, perhaps a little older, and so exceedingly thin that his cheek bones jutted out from his face and his chin was sharp as a flint. He was swamped by an enormous greatcoat of thick grey felt which he wore slung round his shoulders. The hem dragged in the dust.

'Bonjour,' said Ahmed.

'Peace be with you,' replied the boy. Ahmed greeted him again. 'Assalam alaikum.'

'I am Muhadin,' said the boy. 'Muhadin Ali.'

Ahmed said, 'Ali. That is what they call me too.'

'Who are you looking for?'

'I am not looking for anyone. And Ali is not my

name. There is a crazy rich boy, I don't know where he is from, who calls me Ali.'

'It is a good name. Keep it, unless you need to change it for identity purposes. I have other names too. John.' He whipped from a pocket in his greatcoat a travel document and flipped it open to show the holder's name. John William Robertson. And a picture of a fair-haired child. 'I will buy peroxide and bleach my hair when I need to become this John.'

Ahmed said, 'I am looking for a place to live. Are you with your family here and would they have room for one more?'

'No, I am alone. I lodge with an old man in his hut but I travel unaccompanied. I have come from Yemen but I am not Yemeni, before that, I was in Saudi Arabia, but I am not Saudi or Yemeni, I am Somali, my father was killed in the war, so my uncle looked after me in Saudi, when he died, his wife cared for me in Yemen, but she was poor, there was nothing to eat, so I became a slave-worker in a scrap-metal yard, such hard work, but at least my aunt and I could eat, then she also died.'

He spoke like a machine that was detached from these events.

He went on, as if retelling someone else's story, 'And I found there was so much money in her mattress, we need not have been hungry, four thousand dollars, which I took quickly and ran until I found a travel-dealer and I gave it to him. He supplied the documents I need. It was a rubbish passport, not even as good as John, but better than no passport. I will exchange it as soon as I am able. There is always someone worse off who will buy a rubbish French passport. The dealer also provided my train ticket to Calais and I think it is genuine.'

'Calais? Is that a good destination?'

'Not good. Conditions are said to be harsh. But they can be endured. Calais is the final obstacle to be overcome before Wonderland.'

'Wonderland?' He knew his memory was muddled. Could his father and uncle have spoken of such a place and he had simply forgotten where it was?

Ali said, 'It is where I am heading. I have to go there.' Now he did not sound so detached. 'Nowhere else that I have been do I feel at home. To the Arabs I am Somali. To the Somali I am Arab. Everywhere I go I am not part of the community. But in Wonderland, there I will find happiness.'

Ahmed said, 'I want happiness so I can make a home for my mother and my aunts. Where is it, this place?'

'Across the sea in the United Kingdom.'

'Across the sea? There is *more* sea to be crossed?'

253

'It is worth it,' said Ali. 'The English are clean people. They have showers and warm baths. Here, in this quarry, there is no stand-pipe, no well. We have to buy water from the village. No facilities. It is disgusting how we are expected to live.'

Ahmed had no wish to go on the sea again.

'It is a sea in the north but it is not the North Sea. It is known as the Channel. So it is like a canal, not wide at all. You pass under this channel in a tunnel, or over on a ferry. The tunnel is faster. When you are there you ask for asylum. Say you are a war casualty, a victim of slavery, an orphan. Whatever. And then you can work, study, get a good home. This is why it is known as Wonderland.'

Muhadin Ali, who was also known as John, and who may have worked in a scrap yard, may have been Somali, may have travelled extensively in the Middle East and North Africa, and may not have, had a confidence about him. He stood straight, with his head up, eager to get on with the journey. Ahmed was encouraged to see that one can lose everything and still possess dignity.

'Listen, friend,' Muhadin Ali John said. 'Don't ask for asylum in this country. Don't get sent to Germany either. Or Holland. There might be other places that will accept you. But whatever you do, do not remain here. They hate us. They hate any people who are not from here. They hate Arabs, blacks, Jews. Even their own people who come back from Algeria. And the work we can do here is no good. Even if you get the permit, the police harass you. If you want a life worth living, you have to get to Wonderland.'

Ahmed said, 'My father wanted us to come here because I speak French.'

'Doesn't matter. When you get to Wonderland, they'll teach you English.'

Ahmed needed some of this boy's certainty. 'I have a suggestion. We must travel together to your Calais place and we will be safer.'

Muhadin Ali John shook his head. 'Not safer but more conspicuous. These police are wily. They pick you up first, check out their law afterwards. If you have not yet spent a night inside one of their detention centres, let it remain that way. It is because of trouble I have had with other travellers that I travel alone. If you are too afraid to travel alone, you must find another person to be your companion.'

Ahmed knew no people, apart from the obsessive boy with the flags who talked too much, yet told him little of practical use.

Muhadin Ali John said, 'We shall meet up again in Wonderland. One year from now.'

Ahmed had little idea what day it was now. How would he know one year from now?

Muhadin Ali John repeated, 'One year on. At this hour, this day, outside Buckingham Palace.'

Ahmed did not know where that was.

'It is their queen's home and very easy to locate. It is less than one kilometre from where the train under the canal arrives. Their ruler is a Christian but she has a good heart. If my hair colour has changed, if I have become yellow-haired like an Anglo-Saxon, you can be sure you will recognize me by my covering.' He gestured to his grey felt coat with a grin. 'You see, this jacket is now my family. And my security. You too should find a thick coat. At Calais it will be cold. And in Wonderland it will be very very cold. But they will be good to you.'

There was much to learn.

Holy Mysteries

Wednesday was always a half day. Then there was school on Saturday mornings.

Hamish asked Yves, 'But why time off on Wednesday? Why not Saturday so we could have the whole weekend free? It doesn't make sense.'

Yves had no idea. Nor had Pierre. 'You ask too many questions, Oatmeal.'

Luc had a theory. 'It's so young people can relax and not get tired brains.'

Know-all Ned, seeing Hamish mooching disconsolately under the trees on a Wednesday afternoon, reckoned he had the correct answer. 'Hey, 'Omer, don't those guys teach you nothing? Wednesdays, Catholic kids used to go get their catechism from the priest. And some of them still do. But this is a republic. So no religious indoctrination allowed in state school. That's what caused all the carry-on with the Muslim girls and their veils.'

Hamish said, 'I don't know anyone in my class who goes to catechism.'

'Okay, so maybe now it's just an anachronistic leftover, a vestige of holier times.'

Hamish didn't know what anachronistic meant and he wasn't going to ask.

'Hey, don't look so suspicious. It's gospel what I'm telling you.'

'Thanks for the lecture, not,' muttered Hamish, and went back to the villa. But the speaking information centre came too.

'Say, hang on. I was wanting to speak with your mom. Is she home just now?'

'She's busy, exceptionally busy. She doesn't have time to talk to anyone.' Least of all you.

Anne-Marie's
Caterpillars

Extraordinarily, she wanted to go out into the hills and explore.

'Incredible!' he said. He was pleased. 'You mean take a break? Like, not be in the library?'

'Just for a few hours. I have been ignoring you, haven't I?'

'Not specially.' Though she had.

'Chéri, you know I am really sorry I have been leaving you so much to occupy yourself. But this period of the research has been intense. And I have sometimes felt I was running out of time. So now I would like to go out into the garrigue and look for the Thaemetopea pitocampa.'

He knew about the caterpillars of the processionary pine moth. Voracious eaters which, in the days before pesticides, used to destroy entire harvests overnight, leaving the people at risk of famine.

He said, 'But your stuff's not natural history. It's medieval. You get it out of old manuscripts.'

'Yes. Most of it. But the descendents of those maurauding maggots that caused so much trouble for the church and the priests, they're still around. I would like to check on those amiable rogues. Learn what they get up to, see if they still proceed like monks going to Vespers to pray.'

'But you know they'll be just ordinary caterpillars, which will turn into ordinary moths.'

'Nonetheless I would like to view them. To know what type of villain I am dealing with.'

She spoke of the Thaemetopea pitocampa caterpillars in the same way that she used to speak of the sinning pigs, the errant goats, the wayward roosters, as real characters. Her thesis was on the religious trials which domestic animals had to undergo in the Middle Ages. Pigs who'd trampled on crops, goats who'd consumed a washerwoman's laundry, all were held responsible for their actions and sent for trial.

'I hope it will give my thesis greater focus if I have seen the living creatures in their habitat. So will you come with me?'

He'd never been much interested in her stuff beyond that it kept her happy and that, once she completed the doctorate, it would lead to a better job which would benefit them both.

'Please, chéri, say yes. How about next Wednesday and we will make a good expedition of it? And if my sinning caterpillars are too tedious, you could bring a friend.'

Had she been so preoccupied that she hadn't noticed that he had no friends? Not one single pal, chum or companion.

'There is a lad you are friendly with who travels on the bus.'

She must mean Yves. Of course he couldn't invite Yves. Yves had already announced he was going kayaking on Wednesday without so much as a suggestion of a would-you-like-to-come-too.

'Maybe,' he said.

He must not be seen to be totally without a friend. What if he cleaned Ali up, lent him a tidy sweater? He'd pass muster. Though what if Ali proved difficult? He must not refuse. He'd have to be bribed with food. That would certainly work.

Ali wasn't down on the bay and his den had resumed its condition as an anonymous cleft in the rocks. So had he finally taken Hamish's sensible advice?

Hamish set off to the quarry. It was further than he'd

reckoned. He was panting heavily by the time he got there. If you were anxious, panting could easily develop into wheezing. He must not be anxious. At the entrance to their bidonville, the sans-papiers people had rigged up two wooden pallets as gates, topped with barbed wire. Who did they think they were trying to keep out? No reasonable human would want to live in there, without running water or electricity.

Hamish waited by the barrier, hoping someone would come out. He certainly didn't want to go in. They might attack him, rob him. Or even murder him and nobody would know. When he peered through the slats of the pallets he saw their self-build huts, also a thin dog which didn't bother to bark, a fire with a black pot hanging over it and some of the residents who were hanging about doing nothing special.

Hamish coughed, then said, 'Excusez-moi, messieurs.' But, like their dog, they ignored him.

He was about to give up when another man approached along the path from the village, carrying a huge plastic water container on his shoulder. He was dark, with narrow eyes.

'Excusez-moi, monsieur,' Hamish began again. Before he'd said more, the man growled something to him angrily in a language Hamish didn't understand.

Hamish said, 'But I am only looking for someone.'

The man passed through the makeshift barrier into his enclave. Hamish thought he'd gone for good but he was fetching another man from the nearest hut. He spoke in French. 'This is not a good place for you to come,' he said. 'You cannot stay here. Go away.'

'I'm looking for a friend, monsieur. I think he may have come here to live.'

'No boys here. This is not a place for children. We are all workers here. We make no trouble. We work hard. Then we like to rest in peace.'

The Monks, the Bishops
and the Intruder

So the expedition would be just the two of them. He was, after all, glad that he'd have her to himself. He prepared a fine picnic. Baguettes with Normandy butter and jambon d'Avergne, greengages and Muscat grapes, chocolate wafers, mineral water, peach juice.

She applied sun-screen cream to both their noses and they set out along a cool gorge which would lead them to the garrigue.

As they climbed, she chattered about her peculiar research into the medieval animal trials. Her unique discovery was the criminal caterpillars of the village of Cimiez.

When their livelihood was ruined, the peasants had sought the advice of some monks. The caterpillars had been cursed, excommunicated, banished from the region, obliged to live forever in the garrigue, sustained only by the pine-needles of the Aleppo tree.

'And when the Bishop of Nice heard about it,' Anne-Marie, less reticent than usual, went on, 'he summonsed them to court. But they got themselves a virtuoso lawyer. He put up a defence based on the short notice served on his clients. Then he cunningly issued a counter-charge against the peasants of Cimiez. The caterpillars' alleged misdeeds were a divine visitation on the peasants for their own sins. The judge ordered the farmers to fast, to mend their ways, *and* pay a fine to the bishop.'

'Good story,' said Hamish, laughing. 'But it cannot be true.'

'It is all historically documented,' said Anne-Marie. 'Every detail.'

'Monks couldn't really banish insects any more than bishops could send them for trial. Men wouldn't be so stupid.'

'What may seem stupid to one generation can seem morally correct in another,' said Anne-Marie.

'How could a maggot know right from wrong?'

'The conviction that creatures had the same moral responsibility for their behaviour as humans was widespread, not just in this area.'

They paused to rest on a flat limestone shelf under the shade of a pine. Hamish spotted six black and yellow caterpillars straggling along, one behind the other. They were the first Thaemetopea pitocampa he'd seen. They were creepily fascinating.

'Not too good at keeping up with each other, are they?' he said. 'Look at that last one. He's wandering off on his own procession.'

Anne-Marie smiled. 'So perhaps he is the very young novice, with spiritual doubt in his heart? Or is he off to confession for some private sin?'

It was so good that her work was going well and she could be relaxed like this. She made the whole landscape come alive. It wasn't bleak after all. She identified things he hadn't realized were there. 'The garrigue supports such a diversity,' she said. 'Provided one can recognize it.' She pointed out varieties of scented herbs, miniature oaks, junipers, wild lavenders. Talking about what interested her made her light up. He hadn't seen her so enthusiastic in ages.

In contrast to the banished caterpillars, many of the plants were foreigners. 'The African tamarisk, obviously, is not indigenous. Nor the Barbary fig. Introduced from Greece. And the bougainvillea from Brazil. Even the Aleppos came originally from Syria. Now they're everywhere. If the mayor took the same attitude to imported flora as he does to immigrant humans, this entire coastline would become a virtual desert.'

Did she know about the quarry then? Should he tell her about Ali? They were starting a stiff ascent to reach the high plateau when there was an odd yodelling cry. It could only come from one person.

'Hey there you guys! Annie! 'Omer! Not so fast. Where you heading? Wait for me!' Ned was about to join them. He looked dressed for a trek into the Sahara, with a soldier's khaki kepi on his head and his skin whited with zinc sunblock.

From the moment that freaky face appeared, as far as Hamish was concerned, the trip went rotten.

They picnicked on the plateau. Ned was very hungry. Anne-Marie pointed out a black shape wheeling high against the glary sky.

'A buzzard,' she said.

'Gee!' said Ned. 'How do you know?'

Hamish didn't care for the way he had to move so close to her while she described the buzzard's identifying features. He was practically touching her. When they started walking again, he kept scrambling on ahead so that he could lean down and hold out his strong hairy hand to help her.

Hamish said tetchily, 'She's not a baby. She knows how to climb over a few rocks on her own.'

Humiliatingly, it was Hamish who needed help. Dry heat was supposed to be beneficial for his lungs. But there was too much climbing and the ascent was too steep and the air too hot. He had to keep stopping. He kept getting left behind so they didn't go right to the top after all. They picnicked on an uncomfortable ledge which wasn't wide enough for three of them and the picnic things. Ned managed to nudge the bottle of peach juice over the edge. It went bouncing down the escarpment and disappeared into the undergrowth.

Anne-Marie tried to distract Hamish from his growing introspection by pointing out the sea. But though they should have been able to see it clearly from there, they could not. The horizon was blotted out in a reddish haze. The air was becoming thick. It was increasingly hard to breathe. Hamish developed a hard painful cough.

'Use the inhaler,' Anne-Marie ordered him.

She was right. Just a couple of quick puffs of the terbulatine could often prevent the small-scale attack from developing into a major body assault.

But he hadn't brought the inhaler. 'Thought I wouldn't need it,' he gasped.

''Amish in 'eaven's name, what are you thinking? You always carry it.'

'Haven't needed it in weeks.'

Ned said, 'He's got altitude sickness. Air's too thin. Not enough oxygen. He'll breathe easier if we descend.'

Hamish wanted to scream at him. This is not altitude sickness. But he hadn't the breath.

Lower down, the atmosphere was just as oppressive and the air was opaque with the fine red dust. Even Anne-Marie and Ned were finding it irritating. Every few minutes Ned cleared his throat and spat disgustingly into the bushes.

He informed Anne-Marie, 'This is coming in from North Africa. I picked up World Weather Forecast on CBC this morning. There's been storms brewing in the Sahara.'

Hamish gathered enough breath to snarl, 'Storm? Don't be stupid. There's no wind.'

'And ain't that just like the sneaky old sirocco for you! By the time it gets over here, the sea's sucked the power out of it. But that desert dust, why it just keeps on a-coming.' He produced another vigorously projected gobbet and Hamish began to retch.

It was like a vapour, only dry. You could taste the grit of it on your teeth. It was blocking out the sky, not swirling, just stealthily silently coming inland to smother every surface with red. The afternoon sun was all but blotted out, no brighter than a harvest moon yet the heat of it was still coming through.

'Nearly there,' said Anne-Marie, though Hamish

knew there was still a long way to go before they'd even get back to the gorge.

As well as the dust, there were the caterpillars. That first group had been an entertaining novelty. Now they were everywhere. You couldn't take a step without standing on one of their waddling processions and squishing it to a mush which was even more disgusting than Ned's spittle. They were falling out of the branches. They were crawling all over the boulders. Every time you reached for a handhold you couldn't avoid touching them. Their spines left a stinging secretion. Itching, burning, struggling for breath. It was like a nightmare.

He had to have Ned piggyback him the final kilometre back to the Institut.

Recovery Position

He lay on his red-dusted bed with the nebulizer whirring on the chair beside him and the mask over his face. His pillow was smeared with red. It looked like blood. It was desert dust, wetted with snot. It had infiltrated Les Mimosas as everywhere. Table, shelves, books, china, floor, every surface was covered. The windows and shutters of his room were tightly closed but the choking air still got in.

Everything in the outside world was red too. Even the sea was reflecting the rusty sky. And on the horizon, the red crescent moon was drowning.

His breathing steadied gradually. But he still felt crushed as if millions of limestone boulders had fallen onto his chest and were pinning him to the bed. He hated this awful place, really loathed it.

And Ned was still there. He could hear his voice, always too loud. He must be sitting on the balcony with her. They'd be looking out at the strange dim world. They'd be drinking beer straight from the bottles. He hoped they had separate bottles. He didn't want her sharing Ned's.

Eventually, as he was dozing off, Anne-Marie brought him a bowl of soup. It looked thick and creamy until Anne-Marie said, 'It's a chowder Ned has made. He is an excellent home cook.' The soup curdled before Hamish's eyes.

The Convalescent

He was still in bed though he was not precisely ill. Nor did he feel precisely well. He was definitely deeply glum. This mood wasn't helped by the anxious arrangements that Anne-Marie was making for him.

'Dr Whyte understood the difficult situation once I explained,' she said.

The situation, which grew more difficult every day that Hamish was not seen to climb on to the school bus, was that the dependents of Scholars must be enrolled in full-time education, and in regular attendance there, if they were to remain at the Institut. Hamish was no longer in regular attendance. He was still lying in bed.

'He was so kind. He let me use his personal line. I managed to contact the clinic in London. I spoke to the receptionist. She put me straight through to your consultant. He has agreed to fast forward your annual check-up. Isn't that good news? I am so pleased.' If she was so pleased, why was her face so long and sad? Perhaps it was a result of the long night she'd spent on the chair beside the bed, listening out for every breath?

Did he want to be checked over once again by that gang of bronchial specialists in their white coats with their cold creepy hands? The consultant got his subordinates to do the dirty work, to scan him, weigh him, make him breathe into plastic tubes, to draw precious blood from his veins. Only when Hamish was dressed again, would the big-cheese doctor see him, grin, ask how he was feeling in himself. Regardless of Hamish's response, he would explain he had decided to change the drugs.

Anne-Marie went on, 'He says they may need to put you on a short course of corticosteroids. But we won't worry about that till we get there, will we? The side-effects are absolutely minimal. It is an ordeal for you, I know, chéri, going back but it will put everybody's minds at rest once you've been checked over. Now, shall I ask the boy you travel with on the bus if he would bring you some of your schoolwork so you won't feel left out?' She was only trying to be helpful.

'No.' This previously well-focused student no longer wished to keep up with the class. They were being taught the wrong things. They didn't teach you what life was really like. He wanted to be away from this place and was glad that Anne-Marie was seeing to it. Meanwhile she was keeping him prisoner. Like all prisoners, he had to be fed. And as she couldn't cook for him Ned cooked for all three of them. Kentucky Fry. Muffins. Pecan pie. Sloppy Joe. Boston baked beans. Lincoln pudding and litres of his speciality curdled fish chowder. The ingredients came out of packets or cans. Why couldn't he go down to the market and buy fresh?

How the Wind Blows

The region of Provence-Alpes-Côte d'Azur has a climate that is warm, dry and subtropical, ideal for the cultivation of fruits such as figs, citrus, grapes, olives and tender specialist salad vegetables known as primeurs.

He had learned that ages back, under the guidance of Ms Florence.

However, although celebrated for its mild climate, the area is also infamous for its mistral. This is a cold, dry airstream which sweeps southwards from the Alps, down the valley of the Rhône. On reaching the coast it can attain velocities of up to one hundred and thirty-five kilometres an hour. It can also make people go mad.

The mistral arrived with a sudden quickening of the flag proclaiming one of the cleanest beaches between Antibes (population 63,000) and Agde where the naturists gather on the salty flats. The mistral dispersed the African dust clouds, restoring the sky to its profound blue translucency. Apart from that single benefit, it was a mean, twisty wind. It could make itself as imperceptible as a small sharp knife as it cut and thrust, turned and looped. Then the icy blade grew big and twirled anything not tied down into whirling dervishes. It tormented the fishermen, exasperated the harbour cats, flailed the parasols, frightened the birds, devastated the ladies' coiffurs, goosebumped the flesh of the naturist sun worshippers, rattled the shutters, twitched the trees and finally, so they said, sent everybody sane round the bend.

It blew for three days. Even Anne-Marie became touchy, snapping at Ned for rattling pans in the sink, though she resisted snapping at the convalescent.

Weather Forecast

The mistral is confined to this zone between the Alps and the Bouches du Rhône. Snow, however, can fall just about anywhere on earth. In East Africa it snows on Mount Kilimanjaro. In North Africa it snows in the Atlas Mountains. When conditions are right, it snows in the docile provinces of Southern France. Van Gogh is known for painting Arlesian sunflowers and yellow harvests. He also painted the snow-scenes in the same region.

Hamish dreamed it was snowing. The snow turned to sleet, then to hail. He heard the gentle pitter-patter against the wooden shutter. He woke. He went to the window, unhooked the shutter, leaned out into the night. He received a handful of sand in his face.

A voice in the dark whispered up. 'Excuse-moi, mon ami. Je regrette. I am sorry. Forgive me. I wanted your attention.'

'What are you *doing* down there? It is the middle of

the night. Are you quite crazy?' Hamish looked at the luminous dial of his watch. It was just after four o'clock. 'How did you get in?'

'The wall.'

The rear perimeter wall of the Institut grounds was topped with broken glass set in concrete. How could he have climbed over that without being lacerated? Was he bleeding messily on to the white gravel? 'Listen Ali, you cannot, absolutely cannot stay there. No! Do not move about like that. You will activate the security lights. There are electronic eyes all over the place. Surely you can see them? The red dots.'

'Please, friend, come down.'

'I cannot. I have been sick.'

'You must help me.'

How weird. He had never directly asked for help before.

'I *have* helped. I have given you food, have I not? And told you where the quarry is. And let you have a shower. And given you socks and a sweater. What is it now? I suppose it is money you are wanting?'

'I have to travel to Calais.'

'Calais? That's over a thousand kilometres away.'

'Yes. It is far. I cannot go alone. I need your assistance to do this.'

Hamish was incredulous. 'You want *me* to take *you*

to Calais? Why me? You expect me to stop living my life just to look after you? Is that it?'

Ali said, 'There is no one else.'

Hamish said, 'You are ridiculous. You cannot take liberties with me. Go back to the quarry.'

'I cannot. They are clearing it. They have arrived with trucks.'

'Who has?'

'The security. Some of them have guns. The old man I was sharing with told me to run.'

As his eyes grew accustomed to the dark, Hamish could see Ali standing there with nothing but his tee-shirt and torn shorts. He pulled the blanket off his bed and threw it down.

'Maybe I'll see you in the morning. Depends if my mother allows me up,' he said, then he got back into bed two seconds before Anne-Marie appeared like a ghost in the bedroom doorway.

'What is it?' she asked sleepily. 'Were you calling me?'

'No.'

'I heard your voice.'

'Yes. I was talking in my sleep.'

'And you have opened the shutter. Are you too hot?'

'I just wanted some air.'

'And where is your blanket? Are you sure you haven't taken a fever?'

280

'I was shaking it out of the window. It was dusty. I dropped it.'

She looked out of the window. 'I don't see it.'

'Maybe the caretaker found it. He gets up early.'

'Just so long as you're all right, dearest.' She smoothed the sheet round him, kissed his forehead and went back to bed.

He didn't like to deceive her. But it was a necessity. There'd be more deceits to come.

Hamish, the Hero

He lay still in the dark unable to get back to sleep. He did some deep thinking.

Had the boy really forgotten where he'd come from or had he chosen amnesia as a ruse to win Hamish's sympathy? Either way, it had worked. Hamish *did* feel something for him. Not empathy so much as curiosity about his predicament. Thanks to the copious data that Ms Florence used to dole out, Hamish knew that in some places people grew up where there was not enough rain (or else far too much). He also understood, even if this hadn't been something that Ms Florence went on about, that the places with the unstable climates were usually the same places that had political instability, political corruption, civil unrest. Obviously, the boy was one of those people from one of those places. Growing up like that couldn't be easy.

However, growing up was tough for people from safe places too. Just because it rained the right amount so that they got enough to eat, didn't automatically make life a doddle. Because they got a decent education, the well-fed people learned how the world wasn't divided tidily down the middle like an apple. They knew all sides of everything. About rich and poor, black and white, vegetarian and carnivore, war and peace, destitution and indulgence. To have such a broad perspective of the world was not a benefit but a heavy burden.

Hamish watched the silver light of dawn seeping through the window with relief. It was always easier to get back to sleep once you knew the night was nearly over. He heard the first fishing boat chug out to the feeding grounds and the magpies start their daybreak chatter. He lay safe and lonely in his bed beneath his quilt. Out there the boy, scared and lonely, sat on his rock.

He could feel the centre of his being wavering like a magnetic needle seeking true north. He didn't know why. Maybe it was that hormonal activity already happening? All he knew was that he was having some unsettling ideas about change. Muddled but full-size ideas. He wanted to lend a hand in some way. He wasn't sure what way. Then it came to him. He had to do what the boy wanted. He had to save him. He hadn't a clue how to set about doing such an altruistic thing. That was a minor problem. It would sort itself out. The important thing was his certainty that he was the person who could successfully mastermind the salvage. It was going to be a truly philanthropic act and it felt good.

The Collector

He was going to start his new collection first thing in the morning. He knew about collecting. There were collectors' clubs, magazines, conventions. Collectors specialized. Postage stamps, autographs, coins, vintage motorbikes, matchbox labels, sugar packets, Mickey Mouse memorabilia, footballers' sweaty shirts. Crank collectors collected cheese labels and red telephone boxes. Some tried to collect an odd curiosity which nobody else had ever thought of. He had read about a man who started a collection of army tanks but his wife said she would leave him if he brought in any more.

Nobody, as far as Hamish knew, had ever collected a boy.

Boy in the Boot

He knew the boy wouldn't be far but, for just a moment, he didn't recognize him. He was wearing sunglasses with wraparound frames and mirrored lenses which reflected the world in a rainbow glare.

'What on earth is that about?' Hamish demanded. The dark glasses made the boy look shifty, like a dealer. 'I suppose they're yet another treasure you found in some rubbish bin?'

'Yes. But not in a bin. On a bench by the harbour. I must be in disguise if I am not to cause you trouble. I have seen how the rich boys wear their glasses all the time, even when the clouds are overhead.'

'Take them off! You stick out like a pink lizard. Anyway, no one will be seeing you. You are going to have to travel in the car-boot. It is the only way I can think of.'

'You have not told her?'

'No.'

'You do not trust her?'

'Of course I do. But she has a great deal on her mind at the moment. We do not need her involvement until the right time.'

Ahmed-Ali said, 'I am grateful you are doing this for me.'

Every time he said that, Hamish felt good, really good. The hormones must have settled down. The wavering magnetic needle had found its true direction. His inner glow was warmer even than when he'd found the poster for the 1957 version of He Walked by Night.

Ahmed-Ali said, 'I will not ask for much when we arrive. Once arrived, I will disappear from your life. I just want to be able to have a small home, very small, one room only if necessary, where my mother and I can be together when I have contacted her. With a small plot outside for growing a few fresh vegetables, and for keeping a goat and a couple of hens.'

Hamish said, 'Listen Ali, I don't think you quite understand how it is. Britain isn't like wherever you come from. It is quite small and cramped. Loads of people, most people, have to live in flats. There is not space for everyone to have a garden to grow things. Most people have never had a garden.'

'Then how do the people eat?'

'They go to the supermarket.' He was about to add, 'Of course' but held it back. Ahmed–Ali was going to need to know a great deal more about the different way of life of people in Britain. And the only way he would learn was if Hamish told him. Buses, telephone cards, underground trains, compulsory education. Library fines for overdue books. Parking meters. He wondered if Ahmed–Ali knew how to ride a bicycle. Hamish knew. But because of the lungs, Anne-Marie rarely let him out on his own. Supposing, just supposing, they never came back here, but remained in Britain? Ahmed–Ali could be his pal, his chum. They could go biking in the park together.

'Listen, Ali, I am really sorry about not being able to let you sit in the front on the trip. It will not be very comfortable for you. But at least it will be safe. And she is a good driver. She usually keeps going for about two and a half hours between stops. The whole trip from here up to when we reach the terminus will be about ten hours. Or maybe eleven. If there are no hold-ups.'

'Hold-ups? Road-blocks?'

'No. They don't have road-blocks on motorways. Only in American gangster films. I was meaning, traffic congestion or something like that. So, think you can manage it?'

Precious Cargo

What was his alternative? He had none. At the crossings town there'd been tales of youths who had clung for fifteen hours to the undercarriage of aircraft, who'd balanced for twenty-four hours on the metal coupling between two train-wagons, who'd travelled for three days inside refrigerated lorries with no food and no coats.

The boy said, 'I'll make sure there's enough useful things to pad it out. And I'll lend you my watch. It'll help if you know how we're coming along.'

It was not yet light next morning when they met in the parking lot and the boy unlocked the back of the woman's car. Ahmed-Ali peered in. The space was so much smaller than he had imagined it would be. He was having to share it with the spare wheel, a tow-rope and a bottle of windscreen washer fluid.

'Look, I've put the blanket in for you and you can

use my pyjamas for a pillow. And here's some sandwiches I made to keep you going. And a bottle of water.'

Ahmed-Ali took a last glance at the outside world. He saw the shape of the pines against the sky which was lightening to sallow pink in the east. He climbed in. He could lie with his back straight and his legs up on the spare wheel, until the English boy put in a small suitcase. Now there was only one position, curled up, legs crooked round the case.

'Sorry about this,' the boy said. 'It's hers. If I put it inside the car on the back seat, she might get suspicious. But I guess I could take the spare wheel out, leave it behind. Hide it behind the bins. Then you'd have a bit more room. What do you think?'

'No. Leave it. The spare wheel has a significant purpose.' He recalled the saloon car, abandoned, half-buried, in sand. As they passed by the lorry driver had said that seven people had been stranded there when they got a puncture, all for the lack of the spare wheel. Three had perished before the rescuers found them. They'd left the spare wheel behind to make room for one more passenger.

'If you're sure,' said the boy. 'Okay then, it's time. Ça va?'

'Oui, oui. Ça va, ça va,' said Ahmed-Ali impatiently.

290

The sooner this trip started, the sooner it would be over and he'd reach Wonderland.

'See you again at our first stop. Probably about nine. It'll be somewhere near Orange.'

Ahmed-Ali knew Orange. He could see it clearly on Monsieur Bruno's map of the hexagon. The Romans had been there. There was an ancient theatre and a triumphal arch, like the one at Tunis which Monsieur Bruno had visited when he was a young man, long before the troubles.

The boot door slammed shut. He was alone in the tiny space. Darker than the darkest night. The car remained stationary for an eternity. What were they doing? What was the problem? At last, he heard their footsteps on the gravel, their voices. The doors opening, doors shutting, engine starting. They were off.

He had the food the boy had given him, and the water, and the boy's wristwatch. It had a luminous dial. He watched the second hand clicking round. He stopped looking. Having a watch did not help time to pass. An hour or so later when he checked, less than fifteen minutes had passed.

He wriggled in an attempt to make himself more comfortable. He dozed. He dreamed. He watched his mother preparing the vegetables, cutting the mutton, arranging it all on the earthenware dish, lighting the fire, placing the lid on the tajine and the tajine on the heat. He smelled the sweetness of the cumin, the mustiness of the saffron. He tasted the richness of the sauce.

Then he was tossing on the sea, swallowing the water, choking, drowning. He woke to kill that dream.

The stops were as the boy predicted. Every three hours. The second three hours was interminable. Inside his closed black coffin he lost a sense of time and space. When the boy opened the boot, he was blinded by the brightness of the sky even though the sun was not shining.

'Get out now. Quick. While nobody's looking this way.'

Ahmed-Ali couldn't sit up by himself, let alone climb out. His joints were too stiff. They had immobilized him in his curled position. The boy had to assist him out.

Then he propped himself on the rear bumper while he rubbed at his calves and knees. His back ached too. He glanced round anxiously.

The boy said, 'Ça va. She's gone into the shop. And then she'll need to go to the cloakrooms. She'll be a while.'

Ahmed-Ali needed to relieve himself too.

'WC for the men?'

'Best not to go into the building. You could go there, behind the wall. I'll keep watch. If she comes back too soon, I'll head her off to the shop while you hop back in the car.'

When Ahmed-Ali returned from behind the wall, the boy handed him a mug of soup. It was warm.

'Thought you might need something like this. I filled a vacuum flask last night. You still going okay in the back there?'

Ahmed-Ali nodded and sipped. He was glad of the warm drink.

The boy said, 'We're at the Partage des Eaux. Nearly halfway.'

The countryside was smooth and hilly, rolling away like green blankets. The sky was turbulent grey. There was not a tree nor a building in sight, just the seething ribbon of autoroute stretching to the horizon. He had never seen a landscape quite like this. Would Wonderland be like this?

Ahmed-Ali said, 'Partage des Eaux? Dividing of the waters? You mean we are already at the channel?'

'Sorry. Not yet. It's— I don't know the words. In English we call it the watershed. It's where the streams and rivers flow in opposite directions.'

Ahmed-Ali was confused. How could water possibly

flow in two directions at the same time? Had Monsieur Bruno ever spoken of such a contradictory state of affairs? If he had, Ahmed-Ali had forgotten it, like so much else.

The boy understood his bewilderment. He tried to explain it again. 'It means, it's like high-level ground. So that way, the streams will go off towards the Mediterranean. Over there, they run down towards the Atlantic.'

Ahmed-Ali didn't feel reassured.

The boy tried again. 'It means we've got to a good place because the Atlantic is next to the Bay of Biscay. And that's next to the Channel. So we're nearly there. Well, not quite, but we're making good progress. Look I can show you on the roadmap how far we've come.'

He went round to the front of the vehicle. Ahmed-Ali was keeping a watch-out. 'No, not now. She is coming.' He scrambled for the boot. The boy slammed it down on him. He heard the inconsequential pleasantries of mother and son. The engine started. They were on their way. The soup had done him good. He would let himself sleep for the next three hours and hope not to dream.

Train Fever

He said, 'Why did we have to have such a long stop at Arras? You knew we were already behind schedule.'

Anne-Marie said, 'Chéri, I needed a break. Your eyes go fuzzy when you're driving non-stop. I don't know how these lorry drivers manage, keeping going week after week. It's a surprise more of them don't fall asleep at the wheel.'

She never complained about getting fuzzy eyes after reading spidery manuscripts all day long. So why did she have to start making a fuss now? Perhaps she didn't want to go back to London? Perhaps she was going to suddenly change her mind and turn the car round and drive them back south.

'I didn't realize you were going to want to visit that church. You were gone ages.'

'The Saint Vaast Abbey? But I was only in there ten minutes. You should have come too. It was so interesting. They had some relics. At least, that's what it said on the sign. Could have been chicken bones for all any of us know.'

Now she was being flippant to cheer him up. She could sense he was apprehensive. But then she wasn't aware of the extreme significance of the trip. He wondered if Ahmed-Ali could hear them talking. He wondered what it was like back there. Probably not so pleasant. But only another hour and they'd be onto the train, then into the tunnel, through the tunnel, and out the other side. In Kent, he'd be able to let Ahmed-Ali out for fresh air and tell Anne-Marie who he was and hope she'd be cooperative about cancelling the consultant's appointment and driving to Scotland instead.

They were behind two big lorries. Anne-Marie tried to overtake them but the engine wasn't powerful enough. He said, 'What if we don't make it in time? On the tickets it says latest check-in is nineteen hundred hours.'

'I don't expect it'll be a problem at this time of day. But if we don't get there in time, I daresay they'll let me change the booking.'

'I hope so.'

'You're not worried are you, chéri, about tomorrow?'

'Of course not.' At least, not in the way you think.

'It will be fine. Dr Thaxter's a very kind man.'

Folded Limbs

He had planned to sleep as much as he could so as to be alert for what lay ahead. But he could not even rest. Again and again, he checked the time. He could feel by the smoothness of their passage that they were still travelling on a big highway. But they must be nearly at the gateway to Calais.

He considered the variety of ways he had heard of for reaching Wonderland. Every method had its risks. He knew that painful though it was to be folded into a tight space between a spare wheel and a rigid suitcase, he was fortunate. This was safer than the other ways.

The section that made him most apprehensive was travelling through the passage beneath the water for he knew how troubled the sea could be on the surface. However, since the boy seemed perfectly composed about travelling in this way and had done it before, he too must be calm.

On arrival in Wonderland there would certainly be problems. But the talkative boy had assured him he would help. He had to trust him on that. Not knowing the language was an obstacle. The boy had taught him some phrases. He knew nothing of their language beyond the few phrases the boy had taught him. Hello. How are you. My name is. Please. Thank you. What time is it.

The last was stupid. Why would he need to ask the time when he had the boy's watch on his wrist?

The boy had said that once they were in Wonderland, he would no longer need to travel in the confined space, but could sit in the car, provided he fastened his seat belt. They would not go to Buckingham Palace, nor to London. But to a different city where he knew an old woman who might give him shelter for the length of time it took for his application for asylum to be accepted. He would have to go to court. His case would be heard in a law court.

The boy seemed of the opinion that telling the truth was essential. He had said, 'Whatever you do, whoever you are questioned by, speak the truth about what's happened to you. Then you won't have to remember whatever make-up tales you told before and it won't seem as if you're trying to fudge the issues. Honesty is the chief thing that counts.'

It seemed far-fetched and he'd forgotten most of what his truth was. But since the boy was offering to help, he'd go along with his system.

What neither Ahmed-Ali, in his windowless hidey-hole, nor Hamish, in the front seat with full views ahead, knew was that the immigration laws were changing. Not loosening, but tightening. The new government was taking draconian measures to curb the increasing numbers of migrants who were in danger of swamping Britain. Henceforth, all those seeking refuge were to be interned behind bars while their claim was being considered. Unaccompanied children were to be immediately returned to their presumed country of origin.

Perhaps it was as well that Ahmed-Ali did not know what a threat he was seen to be.

Au Revoir,
la Belle France

The final stretch of autoroute was effortless. They sped along at a hundred and ten kilometres an hour.

'Voilà!' she said. 'Pas de problème. We're going to catch it easily. What a funny little worrier you are.' She glanced at him to smile fondly, but did not slacken speed.

Hamish wished he could let Ali know they were nearly there. He'd been in the boot four hours. He must be bursting for a pee. If only they'd worked out some kind of signalling system before they'd set out.

Overhead signs were directing Channel Tunnel traffic around the Calais hinterlands. They were swooping past warehouses, electricity sub-stations, wine superstores with hoardings in English, refuse tips, railway tracks, freight yards. In between, were scruffy patches of derelict land.

Here, Hamish saw the flashes of colour, bright blue, green, grubby white, and knew what they must be. He'd seen similar shelters made from old plastic and tarpaulin in the quarry. These had a look of greater impermanence as if intended for only the briefest of stays.

In their secret flimsy homes beneath the bushes, men were waiting for darkness. Then they would try their luck for the trip of a lifetime. They would move to the roadside, keeping hidden, listening for the sound of an approaching lorry. As it slowed to take the corner, they would slink out and grab for the tailgate, try to keep a tight hold, try to haul themselves on board. Further along the road was a lay-by where unwary drivers pulled over to check their maps, stretch their legs. In the blink of an eye, a man could crawl under the vehicle, and cling upside down to the transmission shaft. Once inside the security fences of the marshalling area they might succeed in getting a new perch directly on the train, balancing on the bogies, squatting on the couplings. By any means, they would reach Wonderland to claim their right to asylum.

And if they failed that night, they'd make their way to the Catholic feeding station for half a baguette and a bowl of vegetable stew, then back to the bivouacs to gather vigour for another try, another night.

As Anne-Marie, Hamish and their unseen passenger neared the tunnel terminus, the metal security fences became higher and spikier. The terrain was landscaped to low neat grass. The carefully planted hedging offered little cover. Hamish wound down his window. He could smell the sea though not see it. He hoped that Ali would realize, by the blast of coastal air, how close they were.

They were guided off the autoroute and along single-file lanes to the ticket check-in. Anne-Marie passed over their tickets and laughed. 'All so easy! We don't even have to get out of the car.'

The clerk inside her glass booth glanced at the tickets. 'Just the two of you, madame? One adult, one child?'

'Oui, merci,' said Anne-Marie.

The clerk issued them their numbered boarding card to stick in the windscreen. 'Duty-free shopping straight ahead. Then follow signs to passport control. Have a nice trip,' she said and waved them through.

Anne-Marie pulled onto the parking area outside the duty-free shopping mall. 'Won't be a moment, chéri. Must go to the toilettes. Or do you need to go first?'

'Non, Maman. Non.' Let's just get this trip over with. Why did she have to keep stopping? This last bit was turning out to be every bit as tense-making as he'd expected.

He watched her go in through the sliding doors. Then he nipped round to the rear of the car.

'Ça va, Ali?'

'Ça va,' croaked the reply.

'Tiens bon. Very nearly there,' he whispered. 'We're just about to board the train.'

He saw Anne-Marie emerge from the shopping centre. By the time she reached the car, he was back in his seat. She placed a bar of chocolate and a newspaper on his lap. 'Thought you might like these to while away the time in the tunnel.'

She started up the engine. The digital departure indicator announced that boarding for their shuttle had begun. She drove forward to join the queue of vehicles waiting for passport control.

Hamish looked at the milk chocolate she'd bought him. Five hundred grams with praline and chopped hazelnut pieces. Excellent. Ali would be in need of quick nutrition as soon as they got to Kent and could release him like a rare species into a wildlife safari park.

He glanced down at the English newspaper. Saw a

headline about the royal family, another about a footballer and his new triplets. But it was the item at the bottom that leaped out at him.

New Fear Over Sanctuary Seekers

Asylum seekers ordered to leave Britain 'disappear' rather than risk being sent home, experts warn. An undercover journalist, who wishes to remain anonymous, revealed yesterday how forty-seven of the ninety-four London-based asylum seekers who had failed in their applications to remain in Britain, had vanished before their deportations could be carried out.

A spokesperson from the Home Office was unable to confirm figures but admitted that 'disappearance' was a growing problem. Unsuccessful asylum seekers are drawn into the black economy and are unlikely to reappear on any census.

Experts at the Refugee Council in London say this state of affairs is likely to be repeated in other parts of the country. Unofficial sources estimate the number of failed asylum seekers who are currently 'in disappearance' to be approximately 20,000.

Meanwhile, immigration officials at Dover have been put on special alert following the discovery of five frozen bodies in a refrigeration truck.

It was scary that this was the kind of news that made the front page. However, passing through passport control turned out to be just as straightforward as the ticket check-in. An official stuck a hand out of the hatch on the glass window of his booth.

'Vos passeports, s'il vous plaît,' he demanded, then changed to English. 'Two passengers? No one else in the vehicle?'

Hamish gripped the sides of his seat, felt himself blush and his windpipe tighten up, becoming so narrow that no air reached his lungs. He was going to explode with the tension.

'No. Just us,' said Anne-Marie.

A couple of gendarmes in navy-blue bullet-proof gilets, each cradling an automatic, stood beside the passport booth. They appeared to be chatting in a casual enough manner, yet Hamish observed how they maintained an unfaltering gaze on the lines of vehicles waiting to be processed. What type of situation would provoke them to stop chatting and start firing? And would they shoot at their own people too, or only at the English or other foreigners?

'And did you pack this car yourself?' the passport official questioned.

'Of course. With the help of my son.'

'Have you left it unlocked and unattended at any point since reaching Pas de Calais?'

'No, we've been driving non-stop since Arras.'

He returned the passports and waved them through. Hamish released his grip on the seat. His breathing returned to normal.

A light drizzle began to fall. The embarcation attendants pulled up the hoods of their fluorescent yellow waterproofs. They were still regulating the flow of vehicles, waving them forward two at a time. What was going on? They'd been through passport control so why couldn't they drive onto the train?

Ahead was a further complication that Hamish had not anticipated.

He had never seen this type of apparatus before. But he knew at once what the security men were doing. They were using infra-red radiation to detect unseen objects. Not just the big transporter trucks and commercial vans but every single vehicle, including private cars, was being checked.

They were only seven vehicles from the inspection point. And that's when Ahmed-Ali would be revealed. The ticket on the windscreen claimed there were two people in this car. The presence of the third would be revealed on their screen.

Hamish grabbed Anne-Marie's arm. 'Go over to the left!' he screamed. 'Now! Over there. Onto the side. Get out of line.'

'What is it?' she said mildly.

'Hurry! You must. Before it's too late.'

She signalled to the car behind her to pass and then pulled over to the side. The saloon on their tail immediately filled the gap. The driver gave a grin of satisfaction. Hamish wasn't the only one fed up with the slowness of embarcation.

Anne-Marie brought the car to a stop in a parking bay. 'My chéri.' She was mixing her languages. 'What is sis matter? Tu es malade? Tu va vomir?'

Hamish gave her a semi-coherent account of the predicament. Her eyebrows shot up in astonishment. 'And 'e is 'idden 'ere, inside sis car? Dans *ma* voiture?'

'I must let him out. He needs to know what's going on.' Hamish leaped out, raced round to the rear, released the boot-door, helped Ali out with some difficulty for he was very stiff, and bundled him fast onto the front passenger seat.

He looked terrible, his complexion yellowish, his eyes huge and dark-ringed.

'Ça va, Ali, ça va. Petit problème. Just a small hitch. This is my mother.'

'Bonjour madame,' Ahmed-Ali croaked in a tiny voice and tentatively held out his hand to her. 'Excusez-moi pour vous déranger.'

Anne-Marie gawped, speechless, then took the hand and shook it. 'Bonjour,' she managed to say. Then, 'Oh, mon dieu. This hand is cold. Like ice. Il est glacé.'

Hamish, now on the rear seat, leaned over to his mother. 'You're not going to betray him, are you? Please.'

'Sere is no betrayal. He 'as done nossing wrong.'

'Parle français, Maman. Or he can't understand.'

She said, in French, 'It is not criminal to seek asylum. It would have been criminal to smuggle an individual through immigration, even if I had been unaware of what I was doing. Since I was not aware, alors, I do not know the legality of the position. But his is clear. He has the right to request refuge and the authorities will see if it is valid.'

Hamish said, 'See Ali, I told you she'd be all right.'

Anne-Marie said, 'But he does not look well. Perhaps he is dehydrated. The first thing is to make sure he is okay. He needs liquid. He needs to eat. After that, we will decide what is the best way to proceed. There will be a solution.'

Hamish was relieved by the calm and confident way she was taking control. She was behaving as he had optimistically described her to Ali, though not as he had necessarily expected.

In No Man's Land

Anne-Marie strode off briskly, against the slow flow of vehicles, in search of a hot drink for the boy and something for him to eat. It wouldn't take long. The tax-free store housed half a dozen fast-food outlets.

The two boys remained in the car. Ali, in the front seat, couldn't stop shivering.

'I did *warn* you about the cold,' said Hamish. 'Don't you remember, I explained that although the climate of the British Isles is governed by the Gulf Stream so it is generally mild, it can also be quite chilly, though never as cold as somewhere like the Alps.'

He spotted Anne-Marie hurrying back across the Tarmac, dodging between cars. In her hands she held a burger carton with a polystyrene cup balanced on top. She was smiling. That was a good sign. He said, 'Looks like it is all going to be all right.'

Ali's teeth were chattering audibly. Hamish pulled off his hi-tog goose feather jacket and gave it to Ali.

'Here, better put this on. I will get my other coat out the back. I will get the rug too. You can wrap it round your legs.'

Ali nodded.

Anne-Marie reached the car. She opened the door beside Ali. 'Voilà. This should help.' She handed him the drink and the burger. 'Soupe aux tomates. Frites et burger.' She wondered if Arabs knew what burgers were.

'Merci, madame.'

He had good manners. That was something. She took off her wet raincoat, shook it, and laid it on the rear seat with her shoulder bag. She scrabbled on the floor for the umbrella. She darted round to the back of the car to shelter Hamish while he was pulling out the tartan rug. Then she handed him the umbrella to hold over her while she opened up her suitcase to look for a thick sweater. Northern France was exceedingly cold compared to the south, almost like two separate countries.

In the few moments that Hamish and Anne-Marie were busy rummaging in the boot, the boy managed to disappear. He wasn't meant to do this, not yet. The disappearing would only happen, if it had to happen at all, after they'd been under the Channel and come up the other side in Britain. When they came round to the front, his place was empty. The hot soup, the burger and chips were still there. The boy and Hamish's jacket had both gone.

Hide and Seek

His initial reaction was similar to his reaction to the sudden loss of the stepfather.

Anger.

How *dare* Ali clear off? After all he'd been doing to help him. It was a betrayal of trust. He'd gone sneakily, without leaving a clue as to his next move, without saying goodbye. Then rage subsided. There came, instead, bewilderment. *Why* had he scarpered? Was it fear that, despite all that Hamish had said he'd do for him, he was in fact going to hand him over? Or was Ali so proud that he believed he stood a better chance on his own? If so, he was truly ignorant of the facts concerning a person already suffering from Post Traumatic Stress Disorder. Hamish knew. He hadn't wasted his time. He hadn't sneaked into the Institute library, risking one of Dr Whyte's scary scoldings for nothing. Crouched on the floor to avoid the electronic eye, he'd thumbed his way through the massive encyclopaedia to confirm the essential facts. If left untreated, Ali's PTSD might become chronic, lead to recurrent minor illnesses, to poor general physical health, in extreme cases to thoughts and acts of self-harm. Even with adequate care, it might take several months for the condition to stabilize.

As Hamish saw it, the likelihood of Ali surviving on his own was slim. He must be found. Hamish pictured what *he*, who did not have PTSD, would do in the same situation. He would calculate carefully, would avoid impulse actions like leaping for the first lorry that came by. He'd go to where there were other people in the same situation. Perhaps the boy would find his way to the encampment on the waste ground? But even if he managed to smuggle himself into the back of a lorry, what would a boy do on the other side if he had no travel documents, no money, no map, didn't speak the language?

Hamish jumped out of the car. 'I have to find him,' he said. 'He can't be far. He won't stand a chance otherwise.'

'Come back!' Anne-Marie called. 'Sis is ridiculous!' She had reverted to speaking English even though they hadn't yet reached England. It was her language for communicating stress and anxiety.

Hamish didn't come back. He ran between the lines

of cars, up and down, back and forth, darting between them, repeating Ali's name.

'Watch it, you young fool!' a driver yelled at him. 'You're going to get yourself knocked down.'

He raced over to where a column of lorries was queuing for the next embarcation.

A British truckie leaned out from his cab. 'Hey sonny, lost your way?'

'No. Lost a person. A boy. Have you seen him, in a red jacket?'

The truck was signalled to move forward before the man could reply. But Hamish had already spotted who he was looking for, a small figure in a big red jacket beside the open door of a stationary car. Ali was about to stow away with another family. Hamish raced over.

It wasn't Ali. It was a young woman throwing a disposable nappy into a litterbin. Her jacket wasn't even the same red. He continued to call and to run. He was dizzy with breathlessness by the time Anne-Marie reached him.

'Come, 'Amish.' She led him back to the car. 'We 'ave to go now. Sis is 'opeless.'

She helped him into the car. She handed him his ventilator. When he was able to speak again, he was still on the same riff. 'We have to stay. He won't have gone far. He'll come back in a moment. We're the only people he knows. He has to come back. He has no other choice. We have to wait here for him.'

Anne-Marie said, ' 'Ee knows *you*. 'Ow can 'ee know me?'

'He saw you several times. And I told him about you. And I said you'd drive him to Scotland so he could stay with Heather.'

'Scotland! Oh 'Amish, why could you not 'ave told me all about sis before? Of course I would have tried to help someone who was your friend. Oh, 'Amish.'

One of the security staff was striding towards them. He was gesticulating and irritated, coming to investigate why a solitary car was stationary when all the rest were being marshalled towards the boarding point. 'You can't stay there!' he called. 'Can't you read?'

Anne-Marie got out of the car, meek and apologetic. She gave a long, emotional explanation, of how her young son had been taken with a sudden respiratory attack, which could even be life-threatening, how she hadn't been able to take the risk of his condition deteriorating while in the confines of the tunnel train.

'He is very very sick,' Hamish heard her say. 'This is why I am taking him to the specialist in London.'

The official seemed more anxious about shifting them off his patch than about the authenticity or otherwise of Hamish's poor state of health. He inspected the tag on the windscreen. 'You know you've missed your departure. This ticket's invalid now. You'll have to go back to the main office, try to get a new booking. I can't see to it here.' He scribbled out a docket for her. 'Take this to the booking office. I can't guarantee anything. You may have to buy a new ticket.'

He waved them through the oncoming traffic flow.

Journey's End

She reparked in an authorized position outside the duty-free shopping mall. She left Hamish with the cup of tepid tomato soup, the cold chips and burger. Obtaining a simple ticket refund was not possible. Getting the same ticket reissued for the next available departure was a laborious process. There would be an administrative surcharge.

'That's all right,' said Anne-Marie. Any price would be worth paying for this nightmarish situation to be over. To get them loaded onto a train, get the train moving, pass through the tunnel, emerge the other side where, despite it never feeling entirely like her own country, she was moderately secure, thanks to her marriage to Douglas. A British citizen with all the rights to which that entitled her.

'Since your delay is due to your son's unexpected ill health, you may be able to claim it back on your travel insurance. Keep all the receipts and send them in with your request,' the booking clerk said with a kind smile. He spoke French with a Yorkshire accent which Anne-Marie found strangely comforting. She wondered if he went back to England every night when his shift was over, or if he lived here in cold northern France.

He pushed a form under the glass partition for her to sign.

Of course she should have realized that Hamish had so much weight on his mind. She should have paid him more attention. She had been too much concerned about his physical health.

The clerk repeated the amount of the surcharge that must be paid before he could issue the rebooked ticket.

'Sank you,' said Anne-Marie and opened her shoulder bag. She found her wallet to take out her bank card. 'May I pay with my card please?' she asked.

'Of course. You have your pin.'

Her card wasn't in its usual slot in the wallet. She felt mildly annoyed with herself. Getting ready to leave Les Mimosas had been a hassle, and she'd been anxious about leaving her computer behind. Hamish had been uncooperative, though now she understood why. At the last moment she'd deposited her computer in the director's office. But she couldn't remember which bag she'd put her bank card in. She must have decided to pack it separately as a security measure. She'd have to use her debit card. But that wasn't in her wallet either.

She'd have to pay cash. But there were no banknotes in her wallet. No euros. No pounds. No dollars. All gone. She searched through her shoulder bag, in each pocket, under each flap. Her passport was not there either. Nor Hamish's. Both gone.

'Excuse me, excuse me,' she mumbled to the clerk and ran from the building with tears streaming down her cheeks.

All's Well That
Ends Well

Hamish in the car had been weeping too. Now he stopped.

'They've all gone?' he repeated. 'Money, passports, everything?'

'Yes.'

Hamish couldn't help smiling. 'So now he has a chance.' He passed his mother a congealed chip.

She said, 'And he's got your best jacket.'

Hamish said, 'So at least he won't be cold.'

They held hands and stared at the rain pattering on the windscreen. There seemed nothing more to say.

Henri

Increasingly, he embraced the French part of his identity. He retained and used the name which Anne-Marie had first chosen for him. He ruminated occasionally about those early sections of his life of which Anne-Marie had been ambiguously evasive. Why had the French bio-father never come looking for him? He supposed the answer might be the same as why he didn't go on searching for Ali. The world was too big, the circumstances too complex.

He continued to attend to his lessons just as hard as he always had. However, the purpose of study was no longer to show that he was the brightest in the class. He was developing a clear, long-term objective. There was a job needing to be done where his boyhood experiences might be useful.

Although he was fluent in French, he chose to study not Modern Languages but Politics, Philosophy and Economics. For his target, he would need a breadth of understanding of the complex workings of the world. At eighteen, he went to university, well focused on the aim of what to do with his life. After graduating, he took a one-year diploma in welfare work.

Meanwhile, Anne-Marie completed her doctorate, and then returned to France. She settled into a small village in Alsace where she became assistant curator, then curator, of the local museum. Henri visited her often but didn't join her permanently.

After his welfare training, Henri was despatched by his superiors to an isolated hamlet in the very middle of Britain, not far from Hambleton Hill. He began work at the Young Asylum Seekers Reception Centre. All unaccompanied minors who arrived sans-papiers, whether at Heathrow, Dover, Portsmouth, Gatwick, or by boat on some lonely Cornish cove, were sent to the newly-built AYSRC for processing. Detention was part of the reception to which they had to submit.

For most child immigrants, their stay in Yorkshire was likely to conclude with deportation. So Henri endeavoured to make their processing as thorough as possible and take as long as possible to give each one of them the greatest opportunity to benefit from shelter, nutrition, health-care, education as stipulated by the UN Charter on the Rights of Children. Henri knew they needed affection too but that was not so easy to allocate. When it became clear that a young person's deportation was imminent, Henri endeavoured to ensure that the individual had been taught sufficient about outdoor survival, had knowledge enough to make his way to a safe house, and knew how to contact a reliable legal adviser. Henri then provided the person with an opportunity to abscond from the detention centre and to disappear themselves into the wilderness of the Moors.

Henri encountered many boys with tousled hair, dark sad eyes and stolen clothes. Most of them reminded him of Ali. Any one of them would answer to the name Ali, or to Ahmed, or Simion, Eil, Juan, Dale, Rojan, Umara or any other name you chose to try out on him. When they'd lost homes, identities, countries, mothers, fathers, sisters, baby brothers, cousins, reasons for staying alive, what they were known by was the very least of their problems.

Henri, as Duty Officer, did what he could for them. And he knew that it was never enough, ever.

BLOOM OF YOUTH
Moving Times Book One

Rachel Anderson

How was I to know that this rambling country Paradise couldn't last? They say we're in the bloom of youth. Ripe for transformation from uncouth savages to marriageable young ladies. But my sister says that out there is REAL LIFE. Bursting with Passion. Love. Fulfilment. We've got to find it.

For young Ruth the future beckons, rich with dreams. But this is the 1950s. There's no halfway between girlhood and womanhood. So where does a schoolgirl seek Life and Hope? Before it slips away, beyond reach?

GRANDMOTHER'S FOOTSTEPS
Moving Times Book Two

Rachel Anderson

I do so much want to follow in her footsteps. On the day the war ended, Granny told me to stick by her and I'd be all right. I'm trying to do just that, to stay as close to her as I can, for ever and ever.

But Ruth's mother, returning from the Victory celebrations, has quite other plans for the family's future. So, in the unfamiliar postwar world, begins a succession of wild schemes, changes and upheavals, different homes, new babies, encounters with strangers. And devastating loss and sadness. But ever present, for young Ruth, is the certain echo of her Granny's footsteps.

STRONGER THAN MOUNTAINS
Moving Times Book Three

Rachel Anderson

Throughout the years that Veritas has spent trying to rear me, there's one essential truth she's always stuck to. 'Love is stronger than mountains.' My mother's name means truth. But can any of us trust her to tell the truth about our family?

As Ruth stands at the altar promising love to this young man till the end of life, under her breath she makes another vow: to set down everything of the past – the reality of a girlhood constantly touched by sadness, yet always profoundly secure.